RYAN'S RETURN

A GRANITE RIDGE OUTBACK ROMANCE

SARA HARTLAND

Ryan's Return
First Published – 2021
This edition published 2021 by Sara Hartland Books
Moffat Beach Qld Australia
Copyright © Sara Hartland 2021
The National Library of Australia Cataloguing-in-Publication
Creator: Hartland, Sara, author
Title: Ryan's Return / Sara Hartland
ISBN: 978-0-6450862-0-1 (paperback)
Subjects: Romance fiction.
Australian fiction.
Contemporary women's fiction.

Cover artwork by Exposed Publishing.
Printed and bound in Australia

RYAN'S RETURN

Romantic Book of the Year award FINALIST

Stranded in the Outback tending her brother's bar after he disappears, Aurora Conroy is battling to keep the business afloat, and her hands off the man who knows her secrets. Her teenage crush Ryan Harrington has secrets of his own, including why he's back in town.

Ryan Harrington knows a lot about success and more about covering his tracks. But when the only family he's ever loved needs him, he's prepared to risk exposure. What he's not ready for, is how hard it is to resist the one woman he swore he'd never touch - his best friend's sister.

(Please note: Ryan's Return uses US English)

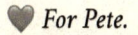 *For Pete.*

CHAPTER 1

"*D*amn you, Davey. Why aren't you answering your phone?"

Aurora's head pounded. When her brother showed up, she was going to strangle him. This was no way to run a business. Thirsty's Bar & Grill was his business, but still. Her money was in it too.

She called out the office door to the bar, "Any sign of the 1:30 appointment yet, Gwen?"

"Sorry, boss. Do you want me to send them in if they turn up?"

Aurora sighed, then yelled again, wincing. "I guess so. Thanks, Gwen." She reached for the ibuprofen packet, popped two tablets, and swallowed them with a swig from her near-empty water bottle. Dehydration was a constant battle.

The deep-throated roar of a motorbike in the street grated on her last nerve. Why the hell did some people think making a racket like that was necessary? Fuming, she rolled her tight shoulders and stood to stretch her back, then walked to the office window, peeking through the blind's dusty timber slats. The source of the rumble was angling back into the curb—a big matte-black motorbike, its rider also in black, both covered in a fine layer of red Outback dust. Aurora's breath caught in her throat.

Broad shoulders, long limbs, and thick chest. Her personal catnip.

Damn, that's fine.

If she was still in Sydney she might have gone outside and tried a little chatting up. The thought made her smile, momentarily. But in Granite Ridge, the gossip that she'd been flirting it up with a bad boy biker would have done two laps of town and been phoned in to her mother before sunset. Her mum didn't need more stress after the horror year she'd had; she needed a holiday.

The engine noise cut to blessed silence. The man kicked down the stand, stepped off the bike, and turned his back to her window as he removed his gloves and full-face helmet, running a hand through his hair.

A shiver ran up Aurora's spine. She'd known only one person with that shade of hair, so dark it was nearly black, and the way it curled at the base of his neck … but no. Ryan Harrington left town without a backward glance ten years ago, two weeks after he'd found her sixteen-year-old self naked in his bed. He'd taken that secret with him, thank God. As far as she knew, he hadn't been back.

As if he felt her gaze burning his neck, the man turned and looked straight at her window.

Aurora released the slats and jumped back before she could see his eyes and be certain.

"I brought you a coffee."

Aurora jumped at Gwen's voice behind her.

"Are you okay, love? You look like you've seen a ghost." Gwen frowned, the lines on her face showing her age as she put the mug on the desk. Aurora noted she hadn't worn the staff polo again; instead her faded chambray shirt was tucked into loose jeans held up with a worn leather belt. Aurora sighed inwardly. Convincing Gwen to accept Thirsty's first ever staff uniform wasn't today's battle, so she let it slide, tucked her auburn curls behind her ears, and slid back into her brother's worn leather office chair, the smell of the coffee making her mouth water.

"No, I'm fine. You just surprised me. Thanks for the coffee, you're a life saver. Has Davey called or messaged?"

Gwen shook her head, her wrinkled face grimacing. "Sorry, hon. I don't know what's with that brother of yours, he used to be so reliable. I'm sure he can't be far away."

Aurora lifted one shoulder and smiled, hiding her frustration and worry. She wouldn't be holding back when she got a chance to set Davey straight. She still couldn't believe he'd taken off on a camping trip without talking to her, so close to the inaugural Granite Ridge Muster in the Dust music festival. He'd left her to run the bar on her own as well as do her festival planning. Sharp words were going to be spoken, and probably a sisterly punch in the arm for old times' sake. But Gwen didn't need to know any of that.

"Yes, he's probably in a mobile phone dead spot. He must have forgotten he set up these interviews. Has anyone else applied?"

Gwen shook her head. "Sorry, love."

Aurora sighed. Two hours of interviews and she hadn't found anyone suitable to help run the pub during what would be Thirsty's busiest ever season.

"Well, I can't waste any more time today. There's so much to finalize for the festival."

"I'll leave you to it then. Yell out if you need more coffee." Gwen's smile was sympathetic.

"Thanks, hon. Can you close the door on the way out? If anyone turns up late, send them in, please."

"Sure thing." The door closed softly, and Aurora slumped in the chair. Life was so much easier back in Sydney. You needed temporary staff, you picked up the phone. God, she missed the city. Coming back home had been the only choice after her brother's accident, but days like today, reality really did bite. She picked up Davey's mug, a memento from some long-forgotten B&S ball, took a grateful sip, and straightened her spine, rolling the chair closer to the desk. Thank God he'd installed a real coffee machine before he'd had his accident. She clicked open the latest version of the music festival run sheet. Yep, when he finally turned up, Davey was definitely getting a punch in the arm.

She didn't have access to Davey's accounting software yet, despite his promises, but with her event experience, she already knew increased sales during the festival could be responsible for a third of Thirsty's annual revenue. That wasn't just a spike in income, it was the difference between survival or not. And it wasn't just Davey's future on the line. Her brother had come to her six months prior looking for help to manage his cash flow, and she'd transferred her house deposit savings to become a silent partner in the business. Their mother didn't know and now Aurora was grateful. She'd had just enough cash left to buy her mum's cruise ticket and cover her own living expenses until she got back to work.

* * *

*R*yan glanced at the shopfront plate glass emblazoned *Thirsty's Bar and Grill* in old-time script. The blinds twitched in the small window next door. He turned on his heel and walked south. Five minutes here and he already felt like he'd never left: wary, watched, and desperate to leave. Small towns. Nowhere to hide. His mouth flattened into a hard line. Give him a big anonymous city any day. He scrubbed his hand over his face. His eyes were dry from the Outback heat and gritty with fatigue. He felt weary down to his bones. Muscles tight from ten hours hard riding complained as he walked out the stiffness. First caffeine and food, then he could face Aurora. He ran his hands through his hair. It was not going to be a pretty reunion.

As he walked, he took note of the changes. Granite Ridge was in serious decline. Empty storefronts stood out like missing front teeth. Only one bank showed signs of life. Maybe he'd done the wrong thing by putting up money to save a pub in a dying town? He shook away the thought. He wasn't investing in the pub, anyway; he was investing in his friend. He already had enough money to last several lifetimes.

Heat from the concrete pavement radiated in waves.

In front of him, the glass door to the butcher shop opened, releasing a welcome blast of cold air.

An elderly woman pulling a shopping bag on wheels bustled out and stopped abruptly in front of him.

He looked down at her and tried to place her face.

She shielded her eyes from the sun with her hand and scanned him up and down. "Ryan Harrington, my, my. Look at you. Are you back for the music festival? You're a bit early."

"Mrs. Bonner." Her name popped up from some recess of his memory. His old music teacher. He'd seen the festival signs up everywhere on the long ride here. "Ah, no. Just passing through."

"That's a shame. You look like you play in a rock band." She chuckled and shook her head. "I always thought you had musical potential, although you were nothing but trouble in class."

Bitterness was a sour taste in his mouth. "Trouble had a

way of finding me then. I doubt the other teachers would have agreed, but thanks."

She made humming noise of agreement, then put a hand on his forearm, her face kind. "I never had much time for your father when he was alive, so I won't lie and say I'm sorry for your loss, but it's good to see you back."

He punched down unwelcome emotion. "Like I said, just passing through."

"I'm on the festival committee and I know lots of people are returning. Stick around if you can."

With that, she shifted her handbag higher on her arm. "The festival is the most exciting thing to happen since I don't know when, and with the drought dragging on, we need a lift. But I've got to get home to Denis and out of this heat. It's lovely to see you, Ryan, even if you're not a rock musician."

Ryan watched her hurry off towards her little car. Her jaunty wave stirred him into action. Coffee first, then find Aurora. The sooner this was done, and Granite Ridge was in his side mirrors receding into the distance behind him, the better.

* * *

Twenty minutes later, Ryan had wolfed down two rounds of toasted ham, cheese, and tomato sandwiches at the only new business he found in town, a funky cowboy-themed café. The Dusty Rose also did a very respectable and spirit-reviving long black.

Afterward, he used their restroom to clean up, splashing water on his face. Eyeing off his three-day stubble, bloodshot eyes, and helmet-mussed hair, he could see what Mrs. Bonner was on about. Definitely more rock muso than Chairman of the Board. But he wasn't here to impress. His face frowned back. More like distress. But it couldn't be helped. He needed to keep to the facts, keep emotion out of it. He was here for Davey. He promised he'd tell Davey's family in person and then he'd be gone. Let the Conroys get back to their lives without him.

Pushing open the door to Thirsty's, he didn't expect the feelings that punched low and hard in the belly as the familiar scent of stale beer hit his nostrils. He looked up, half expecting to see his old man at the end of the bar, scraggy hair, red eyed, and thin, nursing a beer and a sneer. The irony of Davey now owning the pub his father had wasted his life in made his lips twist. His eyes took a moment to adjust to the dimmer light.

An old guy propped up the far end of the bar but didn't look away from the television screen above, where horses were racing live somewhere far away.

Aurora wasn't in the room and he was glad. He needed a moment for the ghosts to retreat before he saw her. Meanwhile, a gray-haired woman behind the bar looked up and waved him over like she expected him. No one knew he was coming, but he was curious, so he wandered over, eyebrows raised in inquiry.

The woman eyed him up and down, a faint frown on her face. "You're a bit late for the interview, but if you go down the hallway, just knock on the third door. The boss is in there and she said you can go straight in." She gestured to a passage in the far corner.

Seizing the opportunity to surprise Aurora, Ryan made himself smile. He'd run a dozen bars like this one since he left and built his empire on turning them into profitable businesses. From the woman's appearance, there was no clue she was staff except her position behind the counter. But she was neatly dressed, her hair in a ponytail, wrinkled face free of makeup, and a faded but clean apron around her hips. The muscles in her sinewy arms showed she wasn't afraid of hard work. From the way she was sizing him up, she wouldn't be one to suffer idiots either.

"Okay, thanks. What's your name?"

"Gwen."

"Hi, Gwen, I'm Ryan. I really need this job. Anything I need to know that might help?"

Gwen looked surprised at the question, but he kept his best disarming smile in place. He'd feel better leaving the place if he knew the staff were trustworthy, especially with the boss away. Things could go pear-shaped quickly, especially in a pub, with the lure of cash in a till and beer on tap to tempt the unscrupulous. The town wasn't in great shape, businesses were clearly struggling. The woman tilted her head thoughtfully.

"It's bar work, not rocket science. Get the job and then we can talk."

He nodded. Davey's staff were loyal. Good. That would make leaving easier. He pointed behind the bar.

"Mind if I pour a beer to take in?"

Gwen's eyes narrowed at his cheek, but after a moment she swung open the hinged counter bench and stepped back.

"Knock yourself out."

When he poured the tap beer quickly with just the right size head of foam, she handed him a coaster.

"She's a stickler for details."

"Thanks, good to know."

He winked at her and she rolled her eyes and turned back to polishing glasses.

At the end of the hallway he paused, closed his eyes, and focused on why he was here. The only good thing about coming back was seeing Aurora, despite the way he'd left, and that wouldn't last when she found out why he'd returned. He squared his shoulders and gave a soft knock on the old paneled timber door.

"Come in." The sound was muffled, but it was the voice he remembered, currently sounding slightly annoyed. He smiled. Same old Red.

Ryan opened the door, stepped inside, and sucked in a breath.

Sweet baby Jesus.

Aurora was bent over on all fours under a table, fiddling with a computer cable, her butt pointed his way.

Her voice came from the under-table space. "Be with you in a sec."

He couldn't reply, his throat tight and dry, air whooshing from his lungs. Blood started to pump fast in his veins, all heading south, which was so wrong. A better man would look away. She was his best friend's sister, for Christ's sake! But then she started to wriggle backwards out from under the table and he knew he was not that man. He couldn't drag away his gaze as her sweetly rounded behind shimmied and flexed under a navy skirt, stretched taut across curves his palms itched to test. Would they be lush and soft or surprisingly firm? His cock swelled to press against his jeans, and he shifted stance, horrified. Now was the wrong time for his body to remind him how long it had been since his last hook-up.

His thoughts remained scrambled as Aurora stood, still facing away from him, dusted her hands against her thighs, tugged down the hem of her skirt, and switched on the printer. She'd cut her hair; the teenage untamed tangle of russet waves hanging down her back was gone. Now well-cut shiny short curls bounced as she moved and revealed the soft creamy skin at the base of her neck. The shorter hairstyle suited her, framing her serene expression as she turned.

Her eyes widened as they collided with his. Her hand flew to her chest.

Those curves hadn't been there ten years ago, either.

But the same wide eyes he remembered, the color of the riverbank moss, stared at him above a lush pink mouth, parted in surprise.

Then her lips snapped closed and tightened into a thin pressed line.

Ryan braced for her spitfire response. Once upon a time he knew what to expect. Red was reliable as the sun rising, the queen of over-reaction. He waited, and it didn't come.

Only her skin gave her away. Her childhood freckles had faded to a light dusting on her fair complexion. A pink haze was already flushing across her chest and making its way to her cheeks. Then another tell, her hands clenching by her side.

There was no escaping it. Aurora was all grown up. And not happy to see him, not at all.

* * *

"*H*ey, Red. I hear you're hiring."

Aurora bit back an oath. Ryan bloody Harrington.

The six-foot-tall chunk of gorgeous manhood slid a beer with a perfect foam head across the desk toward her, on a fresh cardboard coaster. If it'd been anyone else, she would have been in raptures.

"I'm not that desperate," she lied. "And don't call me that. My name is Aurora. I suggest you use it, Ryan Harrington, or get the hell out of this pub." She registered a fleeting look of surprise and something else—respect, perhaps—on the face of the man whose teenage features once haunted her dreams. *Good.* She sure as hell wasn't going to have a repeat of their last encounter, him in control and her dying of embarrassment.

No way. She made herself relax, lowering her shoulders and sitting down in her office chair, looking up at him with carefully schooled features. She'd earned her self-respect. And how to handle herself in awkward situations.

First, get him out of the office. She reminded herself she was a grown woman with a successful career, a string of ex-boyfriends, and a useful grasp of dating apps. She wasn't sixteen and desperate to experience sex with her hero crush anymore. She could do this.

She slid the beer away from her.

One side of his mouth quirked briefly, the gesture an echo from the past that tugged at places she'd thought buried. He wore his hair shorter than his adolescent wild scruffiness, but the same ice-blue eyes stared back at her. He looked tired. He hadn't shaved in a while. She pressed her fingernails into her palms. She was not interested in the least in exploring how that stubble would feel scraping against her palm.

"Seriously, Ryan. What ill wind has blown you back into Granite Ridge?" She regretted the snark in her tone. He didn't need to know he affected her.

He pulled out the worn chair opposite the desk and sat, and her irritation flared.

"I'm busy, Ryan. Davey's not here, if that's who you're looking for."

Something flickered in his eyes, but he glanced around the room as though he was studying it. She resisted the urge to excuse the mess. Her desk was ordered and neat, but Davey's looked like he'd upended a wastepaper basket. She frowned. Things had gotten worse, not better of late, she realized. She'd been distracted, focusing on her timelines for the festival, rather than wondering how he was going with the office work.

"How come you're hiring?"

"Not me. Davey. I'm just covering for him today. Did you not see the massive billboards promoting the Muster in the Dust when you rode into town?" Dammit. Now he knew she'd been at the window looking at him and his bike.

His mouth, the one with the full bottom lip she'd once longed to sink her teeth into, quirked again.

Her belly clenched. She'd been so into his smile back then. She frowned.

Ryan shrugged. "I wasn't paying much attention."

"We're about to be overrun with tourists. This town doesn't know what's about to hit it. Everyone who can work is already employed. Davey had interviews lined up, but half the people didn't show." She didn't add, *including Davey.*

She rolled her head on her shoulders to release the tension building in her neck, leaned back in her chair, then looked at him again. "What are you doing here, Ryan? If you're expecting to see Davey, get in line. He's overdue back from a camping trip, and his timing is terrible."

"Actually, Aurora, this isn't a social call."

Something in his tone of voice and the lines of worry between his eyebrows sent a chill skittering down her spine.

He inhaled before appearing to choose his words with careful consideration.

"I'm here about Davey. He asked me to let you know that he's okay, but he won't be around for a while."

Sirens sounded in her head and the steel band gripping her chest tightened. Davey and Ryan were once best friends, but as far as she knew, they hadn't been in touch in years. Foreboding flooded her veins with ice.

"What do you mean? What the hell is going on? Is Davey in trouble?" Her voice was shrill.

Ryan's jaw clenched and he looked away. When he looked back, his face was a shield, expressionless when he answered.

"Davey's checked himself into a drug rehabilitation clinic near Byron Bay."

His words were a bomb detonating.

"Don't be ridiculous." The words exploded from her lips. "Davey doesn't do drugs."

Ryan didn't respond, his gaze steady, his body unnaturally still, like he wasn't even breathing. Was he made of stone? Fury ignited. At Ryan, at his preposterous words. What could he know? The whole idea was ridiculous. She wanted to leap up and attack him with her fists like she was ten and he and Davey had played a trick on her. Fury spiked. She got up and paced, shaking her head.

"Davey isn't like that. He wouldn't. I'd know." She jabbed a finger at him. "You're wrong, Ryan."

She saw a flash of pity in his eyes. And just like that, doubt began, seeping in and spreading its toxic poison. What if *she* was wrong? Aurora grasped the edge of the desk as her stomach roiled. Spots formed in front of her eyes and she couldn't take in air.

"Are you okay? You've gone pale. Shit." Ryan leaped around the desk, pulled out her chair, pushed her into it, then crouched beside her. "Put your head down between your knees and breathe, Red." His deep voice was gentle, his hand on her shoulder firm, its weight grounding her when she felt like flying apart at the seams.

She'd nearly lost her mum to cancer, Davey's car accident, and now this? It couldn't be real. Aurora squeezed her eyes against tears and tried to take a breath, but only a hitching gasp sounded. No air was going in. Then she registered the warmth of Ryan's palm, sliding up and down her spine.

"You've got this, Red. Slow deep breaths, like you're blowing out a candle."

His hand was light, soothing, his voice calm. And it helped. His touch was definitely distracting. She managed a shaky slow breath or two, and then finally a shuddering sigh.

His fingers lifted the moment he sensed her recovery.

She was grateful, even as a part of her mourned the loss of contact, her breath still ragged. She concentrated on calming herself. She could not lean on this man. Anger flared, at herself for losing control, and at him.

"Stop. Calling. Me. Red." She opened her eyes to glare at him.

He was too close and saw too much.

Their gazes locked.

She remembered the last time they'd been this close. She was so sure she'd read an answering heat in his eyes. But then he'd thrust her clothes at her and turned away. He hadn't wanted her, and his words then still echoed in her head: "Get dressed, Red. This isn't happening. I'm taking you home, now." The sting of rejection, the raw hurt. She closed her eyes, shoved the feelings away. *Not today.*

Maybe he was remembering it too because he looked away and pushed back to his feet, returning to his chair. "Sorry ... Aurora."

They sat in silence. Aurora's heart rate started to come down, but her stomach churned. She chewed her top lip as she thought about Davey's behavior in recent months. Guilt ate at her. How had she missed the signs? He'd always been overprotective. Maybe he'd just hidden them so she didn't worry?

"But why are *you* telling me this? I didn't realize you two were still in touch. Why didn't he tell me himself? Can I talk to him?"

Ryan shook his head, his eyes sad. "I haven't seen him. I think he's just dealing with it as best as he can. He didn't tell me much. He asked me to tell you he loves you, he's sorry he didn't tell you first, but he just had to go. He'll call when he can, but it may not be soon."

"Does Mum know?"

Ryan shook his head. "Not yet. I'm going to see her next. I know it's been a tough year. How is she now?"

Aurora sighed. "She's well now, thank heaven. She's leaving in two days to go on a tropical cruise with her friend Penny."

"Good for her."

Her stomach took another dive as reality hit like a smashed smartphone.

"Oh God! She's going to freak out! That's the last thing she needs at this stage of her recovery. She won't want to go now."

She turned her gaze to him and saw the truth of her words written on his face.

"Ryan, she has to be on that ship."

CHAPTER 2

*A*urora looked stricken and as pale as she had when he dropped Davey's bombshell. The freckles he'd always liked, but she'd cursed as a teenager, stood out on her creamy skin.

He resisted the urge to cover her hand with his for reassurance. She'd probably bat it away, anyway. They both knew the truth—Rosemary Conroy wouldn't get on that ship without some powerful persuasion.

Aurora's eyes were beseeching, and he felt himself wanting to solve this for her. Her chin dropped and her shoulders slumped.

"Mum really needs that cruise. The chemo knocked her around. The doctors have cleared her and the boat leaves from Sydney in two days' time." She stared at him miserably, arms wrapped around her torso. "How the hell am I going to convince her?"

"Let me help you." The words sprang unbidden and he wanted to take them back, except he knew in his bones they were the right ones.

The Conroys were good people. He owed them everything. Rosemary had seen past his teenage walls, nourished him with food and kindness, and given him hope for a better life somewhere else. He could never repay her or Davey. When his old man stole his meagre savings and blew it on a binge during his last week of high school, his friend sold the motorbike he'd worked odd jobs to save for and forced the cash into his hand, along with a bus ticket out of town. Ryan repaid him within months, but his friend's faith in him had been the push he'd needed to escape. The chance to help now in return was a gift.

"She might listen to you." Aurora scowled and Ryan bit down on a smile. It would have hurt her to admit that. Her brother and mother had a blind spot about Aurora. They tended to underestimate her. It drove her bananas, an over-protective habit because they'd lost her dad in a car crash when she was two.

"She might," he agreed. "Do you want to go and see her now? She'll need time to process the news and be talked into going."

"You're right." Aurora blew out a breath and gave him a grateful look. "Thanks, Ryan." She picked up her handbag and found her car keys. "We'll take my car."

* * *

*G*wen looked curious as Aurora came into the bar, car keys in hand and Ryan following, but she didn't ask questions.

"I'm just ducking out for a bit, Gwen. Hold the fort, okay?"

"Sure thing."

In the rear car park of Thirsty's, she beeped her keys and the lights on her little Mazda flashed. It was going to be a squeeze for Ryan, but he didn't complain, just moved the seat back to make room for his legs. Prickles of awareness began tingling in all her feminine places. If she wanted to, she could reach over and put a hand on his thigh and feel the strong muscles under the worn denim. She kept her hands busy instead, cranking the air conditioning to cool her car and her skin. As he settled in the seat, his scent enveloped her, and the tingling turned into more heat, her nipples hardening. He smelled like a man, a faded hint of some spicy cologne, mixed with sweat and dust.

His door slammed closed and a memory returned with the sound: the last time they'd been in a car together. Ten years ago, a moonless dark night, Ryan driving his dad's unregistered battered sedan with the lights turned off. Returning her home via the back streets after her humiliating seduction failure. The rattle of its loose muffler scraping her nerves, wanting to cry but still yearning to reach out and touch him, silence between them, her heart aching and confused. She'd been so sure. How had she gotten it so wrong?

She refused to think about it today, and she didn't want him to either. She turned onto the main street, for once relieved to find it so quiet. She didn't want to be answering questions later about who was in the car with her.

"My head is still spinning with the idea of Davey abusing drugs and putting himself in rehab." How had she not seen any signs?

"Same here. After he called me yesterday, I made some calls. The place checks out, if that's any comfort."

Another thought hit. "What is he being treated for? Is it Ice?" She held her breath. She had friends in Sydney into the party drug scene, but she fervently hoped it wasn't Ice, the scourge of small communities in the bush. The chance of accessing support services to help recovery out here would be grim.

She glanced at him and Ryan's fingers curled and released on his thighs. He was looking out the window as the streets rolled by, but she couldn't see his eyes behind his sunglasses. He wasn't smiling.

"I honestly don't know. We didn't talk long. I'm sorry I don't have more answers."

She drove through familiar streets and wondered what he was thinking. He'd barely been back, as far as she knew. They'd be at her old family home within minutes. Something else bothered her.

"Why are you here? You could have just called."

Ryan was silent. She thought he wasn't going to answer and then finally he spoke.

"I promised Davey. I owe him."

She glanced across. His face was turned away, the muscles on his jaw working like he was dealing with some demons of his own.

As she turned into the street she grew up in, she eyed her mother's modest white stucco house with its faded blue roof. Nothing had changed here in ten years. Same rose garden, same front patio, same simple gravel drive to the pitched-roof iron shed that served as a garage behind the house. Her knuckles turned white where she gripped the steering wheel and the car slowed to a crawl.

"Your mum is tougher than you think. She can handle this." Ryan's voice was gentle.

His kindness nearly undid her, and she clenched the wheel harder, the tightness in her throat an ache.

"How can you be sure? No mother wants to hear what we have to tell her. And we don't know anything!"

"I phoned the center and talked to the management and I did some online research. It's the best place in Australia. That's what I'll be telling her. Your mum will take her cue from you. You've got to be the strong one for the family now. You can do this Aurora."

Pulling into the driveway, she blew out a big deep breath and stopped the car, then turned to look at Ryan. Last time they'd been this close, he hadn't said what she needed to hear. Today he had. Perhaps they'd both changed.

"You're right." She nodded. "Thanks, Ryan. Let's go."

The front door was open.

"Hey, Mum, where are you? I've got a visitor for you," she called out as they walked in.

"In the kitchen, love. I'll put the kettle on."

Aurora stepped into the kitchen first and watched as her mum's face lit with surprise and then delight as she realized who her guest was, and then flew across the room to Ryan, who wrapped her in a hug. With her post-chemo pixie hair-cut, she looked so tiny and fragile in his big arms, and it was so sweet, and their news was so horrible … Aurora swallowed hard.

"Oh, you beautiful boy! Ryan, you should have let me know you were coming!" Her mum beamed and released Ryan, bustling to set out cups for coffee. "This is the best surprise ever."

Aurora glanced at Ryan and he gave her a tiny nod. The twisted knot of tension in her stomach eased a little.

Rosemary kept up a rush of chatter as she made them all coffee and then joined them at the scuffed kitchen table.

When Aurora couldn't bear to wait any longer, she drew in a fortifying breath and placed her hand over her mother's fingers.

Rosemary looked up in surprise.

Aurora pressed on, ignoring her own heart breaking as she delivered crushing news to the person she loved most in the world. "Mum, we have some news about Davey."

The blood drained from her mother's face, making her paler than she'd ever been on the worst of her chemo days.

Aurora rushed on. "He's okay, he hasn't been in another car crash, but … he's booked himself into a drug rehabilitation center out on the coast."

Her mother seemed to shrink in on herself. Her eyes welled and she closed them, sucking in her lips and pressing them tightly together as though holding in a wail of denial. Her chin lowered and tears started rolling slowly down both cheeks until they reached her jaw and fell to her floral blouse. Her head shook slowly back and forth.

Aurora choked back a sob as her tears started again and squeezed her mum's hand.

Her mother placed her hand over the top of Aurora's, rubbing her skin, her response to soothe automatic.

As much as she hurt for her brother, it was crushing to watch her mother suffer. She suddenly understood why her mother had tried so hard to shield her over the years. She'd have done anything to shelter her mother from this pain, but all she could do was sit and be with her as she absorbed the news. Beside her she heard Ryan sniff and she couldn't look at him, risk seeing him undone too, or she'd lose it completely.

They sat there, the kitchen clock ticking loud in her ears, until her mother opened her eyes and released a sigh that came from her whole body. She released her hands and fished in a pocket for a tissue to wipe her eyes and then blew her nose.

Aurora rose to grab the box of tissues from their place over the fridge, putting it between them on the table and mopping at her own eyes.

"Thank you for telling me in person." Rosemary managed a tremulous smile at both Aurora and Ryan. "Have you seen him, Ryan?"

"No. He called to explain where he was and asked me to come and see you."

After that, they talked about what little they knew. Ryan reassured them about the place where Davey was and that the cost was being covered. Aurora wondered how and made a mental note to ask him later. He revealed that Davey wouldn't be able to contact anyone for at least the first two weeks while he settled in.

That explained the unreturned calls.

"We didn't talk for long. I said I'd see you both in person. He was terribly guilty about the timing, but I did all I could to reassure him that everyone would just want him to focus on getting well. Rosemary, he was also adamant that you should go on your cruise. He made me promise to make sure you go."

It was a lie, but Aurora felt a surge of gratitude.

Rosemary shook her head. "Oh, I couldn't possibly go now."

"Oh Mum, you have to!" Aurora cried. "It's all paid for. You'll just go crazy worrying if you stay here. At least on the cruise you'll be distracted. Please go. You need this."

"Oh no." Rosemary shook her head. "You'll need support Aurora, covering for Davey and everything else you've got on your hands with the music festival. I've seen the hours you're putting in on the computer and your phone never stops buzzing. It's too much. I can at least cook your meals and make sure you have a bed to fall into until it's over. I'm staying."

Aurora strove to keep her voice calm and reasonable, hiding her turmoil.

"Mum, I'm already settled at Thirsty's, and what about Penny? She won't go without you. You've both wanted this for so long. She'll be devastated."

"Penny can still go; her sister might be able go in my

place." Her mother looked conflicted, but her words and voice were firm.

Aurora looked at Ryan, raising her eyebrows and widening her eyes in a plea for him to jump in.

He just lifted a shoulder.

Some bloody help he was.

"Mum, I need you to go on the cruise so I can focus on work. I can handle this. Events are what I do. My old boss knows that, which is why he gave me extended leave to come home when Davey had his accident." She resisted reminding her mother she'd have been home sooner if Rosemary and Davey had been honest about her mum's cancer. That wound was best forgotten. "If I know you're prioritizing your recovery, it will free me to keep my mind on the job."

Rosemary chewed her lip but shook her head, and Aurora's anxiety kicked up a notch. How could she get through to her?

Ryan's chair scraped as he shifted in his seat.

"What if I stay and help Aurora with Thirsty's?"

Ryan's offer sucked the oxygen from Aurora's lungs. She stared at him in wide-eyed shock. *This was his idea of helping? There was no way she could work with him.*

His face was as serious as a heart attack. He wasn't joking. He threw her a quick look that said, 'just go with me on this'.

Her mother stopped biting her lip and looked interested.

"Could you do that? Aren't you working?" she asked.

"Yes, but it's my own business. My assistant is always telling me I'm overdue to take a holiday. I can swing it. Plus, I'd get to hang out with Aurora." He smiled at her, as if daring her to contradict him.

Aurora wanted to gag but managed a weak smile. Working with Ryan was a bad idea. The worst. The possibilities ranged from mildly awkward to excruciatingly frustrating. She'd obsessed about him as a teenager, but ignoring the raw sex appeal of the fully grown male he'd become would be torture. But she couldn't let the pub fail either. Davey needed her and she'd never let him down. And if agreeing to let Ryan help got her mum on that ship, she had no choice but to play along, for now.

"Hmm. It'll be ... nice," she managed. *Lying is harder than it looks.*

It was enough to convince her mother.

"It's a lot to ask Ryan, but if you're sure? It might help Davey to know you're here."

Aurora wanted to scream with frustration. But this wasn't about her, and there might be a nugget of truth in her mum's response. Davey had reached out to Ryan, not her, she noted bitterly.

"If you cook me corned beef for dinner tonight then the deal is done. I stay until Aurora doesn't need me." He raised his eyebrows at her, and the glimmer of a smile teased his lips.

Aurora narrowed her gaze at him. She didn't need him now, but she bit her lip hard. Her mother was her priority. She'd take care of Ryan later.

Rosemary was finally looking a little brighter. Aurora tried not to take it personally. Her mother had lived her whole life in a small country town—she really didn't comprehend her daughter's skills and experience, not matter how proud she was of her. She suppressed a sigh as her mother patted Ryan's hand.

"If you're here, that will give me some peace. Thank you. Thank you both."

Aurora could only smile on the outside and wonder how in hell's name she was going to stand the next few weeks running the pub and the festival. One thing was for sure, it would be without Ryan's help. Once her mother was on that cruise, she'd kick him to the curb.

CHAPTER 3

*T*he bike was still there—dark, powerful, and sexy, just like its owner. Aurora peeked out her office window for the third time in an hour and sighed at the cute couple leaving Thirsty's together, holding hands. She was happy her old school friend had found love. Jazzy Parker was the youngest mayor in Granite Ridge history, its first female head of council, and she'd found the love of her life in the hospital's new medical superintendent, Irishman Dermot Flynn. If that wasn't proof miracles could happen, even in this dusty backwater, nothing was.

Eyeing the first star of the night sky, Aurora crossed her fingers and wondered if wishing on it would help. Not for romance obviously—she needed that like a hole in the head. She closed her eyes and wished hard for Davey to come back home safe and well soon, recovered from his addiction. Nothing else mattered.

A figure stepped out of the shadows, and her heart rate spiked. In daylight Ryan had been commanding, in darkness with the bar's neon sign-writing casting shadows on the angles of his jaw, he made her breath hitch and her skin prickle. He strode over to his bike and she drank in the sight of him gliding his hands carefully over the machine, her mouth drying as the denim tightened on his butt when he crouched to inspect the tires.

His bad boy edge drew her in. But others saw him differently. He was the apple of her mother's eye, her brother's one-time best friend. He'd done the right thing by them both. She crossed her fingers that he would do the right thing by her. And that meant getting the hell out of town the moment her mother left. She couldn't risk him guessing her secret: her wild teenage crush hadn't passed. It had just laid dormant waiting for him to ride back into town on his big black motorbike looking like every bad girl's wet dream.

She needed to corner Ryan alone outside so she could tell him exactly how things were going to be, without worrying someone might overhear her and blab to her mother. Secrets were damn hard to keep in small towns.

Grabbing her bag, she left the office, locking it and saying goodnight to the bar staff who'd work through 'til closing. She hadn't reached the front door yet when Ryan strode through and blocked her exit.

"Hey. Glad I caught you. Can I buy you a drink?" His calm demeanor gave nothing away, but the lift of his chin hinted that he wouldn't be dissuaded.

"Actually, I was just leaving. It's been a long day. How about we chat outside?" She tipped her head subtly at the bar staff, about ears listening, so he'd get the hint.

He just quirked up one side of his mouth. He got the hint; he just refused to go along with it. "A quick drink won't take long, I promise. What do you like? White wine?"

Aurora huffed out a breath. She wanted this meeting done. "Oh, all right. Sav blanc for me." She eyed the bar room and pointed to a vacant booth right at the back with no tables occupied around it. "I'll be down there."

His eyes glittered with amusement. "Gracious as ever. Make yourself comfortable. I'll be there in a minute."

Aurora rolled her eyes and stalked away, the worn carpet absorbing the stomp of her sneakers. Coming home was a bitch. Everyone thought they knew her so well. They didn't. She'd changed. Ryan needed to know she wasn't a kid he could dismiss any more. It would have been so much easier if they'd run into each other in some bar back in Sydney. She would have been in her chic corporate wear for a start: elegant and classy, heels, makeup on point; not as she was tonight: makeup free, a quick-dry staff polo untucked over a plain navy work skirt. She thought about applying a coat of her favorite red lipstick but quickly dismissed it. She didn't need its confidence-boosting powers, she lied to herself. Plus, Ryan would notice and draw the exact conclusion she didn't want, that she'd done it for his benefit.

Sliding into the booth, she sat where she could keep an eye on the room and ensure their conversation remained private.

Ryan was chatting animatedly to the barman, Ant, and Aurora's senses prickled.

She'd need her A-game to keep ahead of the man talking. She wasn't the only one who'd changed. He used to hang back, let Davey take the spotlight. But now, Ryan radiated command. The shift was subtle. It had nothing to do with the way he looked, more in his bearing and quiet confidence. Perhaps her mother had responded to that. Whatever it was, it rubbed Aurora the wrong way. She was in charge. A prickle of unease slid up her spine. Why was he taking so long?

Now Ant was talking. The barman was a gentle giant who rarely strung two words together, but he was animated as he spoke to Ryan.

Did everyone fall under his spell? Curiosity burned. What were they saying?

Finally, Ryan gathered their drinks and stalked toward her with a cat-like grace that was at odds with his height.

Her pulse kicked and she straightened in her seat, tension on the rise. The sleeves on his black t-shirt strained around his biceps and his dark jeans rode low on his hips. Her eyes were drawn to the worn creases at his crotch. She dragged them upward and he caught her perusal, his eyes glinting. She swallowed, her throat dry and her heartbeat stepping up a notch. Did he have to be so sexy?

He sat down opposite her, ice clinking in his tall glass of cola as he placed it and her glass of wine neatly on coasters.

She bit her lip to stop interrogating him about his conversation at the bar, but he read her mind.

"Your barman said he last heard from Davey a week ago, a text that said he was visiting a pub run by an old friend. It gave me an idea that gives us a cover story."

Aurora held up her hand and he stopped.

"There is no 'us' Ryan. There's just me. I've got this. After Mum leaves, you can just get on your bike and ride off without a backward glance."

Again.

The word wasn't spoken, but it hung in the air between them.

He tilted his head.

Her throat was tight. She wished she could take back the words. They gave her away. The hurt sixteen-year-old version of her, who felt somehow responsible for his leaving.

Ryan was frowning.

"Is there a problem?"

"Sorry. That sounded … judgmental." She winced. "Truthfully, I'm not much better. I'm here for a few months more, but when Mum's fully recovered … and Davey … I'm going back to my Sydney life."

She took a sip of wine and raised her eyes to his. "Thanks for helping me persuade Mum, I really do appreciate it. Coming here in person was very kind. It softened the blow for Mum and I'll always be grateful for that. But you've done enough. I can handle things from here."

Ryan raised his eyebrows briefly and moved his drink to the center of his coaster, then sat back in his chair, one side of his mouth lifting.

"In a hurry to get rid of me, Aurora? I just got back. I'm sticking around; you might as well get used to the idea."

He was baiting her. What possible reason could he have for staying?

"Why?"

"I promised Davey. I promised your mum. I always keep my promises."

He stared at her then, like he was daring her to read his mind.

Aurora's heart kicked and electricity zapped in the air between them. He was stating some intention, but did he mean what she thought? Desire sparked, despite her efforts to quash it.

"Surely you have things to get back to?" Her voice sounded breathless.

"Surely you can accept you need help?" he countered. "Face it, Aurora, you're desperate for staff. I'm here—ready, willing, and able. You've got a music festival to pull off. The pub won't run itself. You can't do both. I've run a few pubs. If you've got a better solution, let's hear it."

And just like that the air whooshed out of her lungs and bile rose in her stomach.

"I'm here, and you're desperate."

It really shouldn't sting.

The gleam in his ice-blue eyes gave it away. He was enjoying toying with her.

Bastard. Damn him for being right. It was time to pull on her big girl pants and accept the help he was offering, for now. Imagining them granny style and beige instead of red lace and Brazilian cut helped.

"Fine. If you're so determined, you can prove it tomorrow. Davey was rostered on for the morning shift. Can you be here at 8:00 a.m.?"

At his nod, Aurora got up to leave, sliding her bag over her shoulder. "I'll see you then."

Ryan raised his eyebrows. "What, not staying to finish your drink?"

"Don't worry, you'll be seeing more than enough of me the next few days."

She bit her cheek as she realized what she'd said. Ryan had already seen her naked.

His soft laugh followed her as she walked away, head high, but cheeks aflame.

* * *

*R*yan elbowed the caravan park cabin door closed, dumped his helmet and backpack on the worn pine table and fell into the embrace of the saggy sofa, phone in hand. "I'm not coming back until the board meeting."

"What do you mean?" Tracey scoffed. His executive assistant thought he was joking. He could relate. He could barely fathom it himself. But he couldn't ride off and leave Aurora to manage Thirsty's as well as an event that could save this godforsaken miserable drought-ridden town. Not when he was uniquely placed to help. HLR Group could spare him for a few days. He'd be back for the board meeting the week after the festival. He could stomach Granite Ridge for that long.

"You haven't taken a day off in three years," she stated.

He smiled. "You make me sound terribly dull."

She huffed. "No one would ever accuse you of that. This is just out of character. Have you been taken hostage? Cough twice for yes. Where are you? Please tell me it's somewhere exotic and relaxing."

"It's a little place in the Outback."

"Oh, be serious. Is it Bali? The Maldives? I know, Japan."

He laughed. "No, it's Granite Ridge. It's not the end of the earth, but you can see it from here."

The phone went silent. "Well that's quite … unexpected. What on earth for?"

Tracey knew more about him than anyone, and she didn't know where he came from. He'd trained her to be uncurious about his personal life and past history and protect his privacy. She was adept at screening calls, especially from persistent women who wanted more than he was prepared to give, which was anything longer than three dates. It was a perfect working relationship. He knew all about her family life, but she understood it was a one-way street.

"I fancied a road trip."

"Alone?"

"Of course. Any concerns I need to know about?"

"No. Everything is going smoothly with the new acquisition, though one due diligence report hasn't come in yet. Oh, and Chantelle is still calling. She insists she needs to talk to you, and only you. She's quite adamant."

He merely grunted. He had nothing to say about, or to the woman. After catching her snooping through his desk, he'd made it clear that they were over.

"Email that report as soon as it gets in. I'm checking emails. Block Chantelle."

"Fine. Are the natives friendly?"

He thought of Aurora and her green eyes flashing fire as he manipulated her into going along with his plans thus far. "Hmmm. Let's just say they're warming to me, slowly."

Tracey chuckled. "You could be charming if you tried. Give it a go, you might surprise yourself. Just don't meet any nice country girls. It wouldn't be fair. They'd fall in love and just get their hearts broken."

The truth held a sting. Something inside him responded to Aurora, always had; but he was in control, and he'd never risk his relationship with her family to test if she was the one who could force a beat out of his stone-cold heart. Didn't mean he wasn't tempted. The flare in her eyes today showed him she still felt it too. But she deserved more than he could offer. You had to have known love to be able to give it. Sex, even fantastic sex, would only mess things up. No, he and Aurora could only ever be friends. He'd enjoy spending time with a woman who didn't see him as a meal ticket or a trophy to collect. He'd keep his hands to himself, help her out, and then get on his bike and leave, just like she wanted. It was for the best, wasn't it?

"Excellent advice. I'll be in touch."

CHAPTER 4

"*H*ey, Aurora. Keepin' busy?"

"Always, Gareth. What brings you into town on a weekday? Kind of early for beers, isn't it?"

The cow cocky fidgeted with his battered Akubra. The sweat-stained hat had seen better days; the crown had a tear in the felt and the brim was misshapen. He smirked at her, and she fought to hide her repugnance as he scratched at a scab on his chin.

"Thought you could do with the business. Haven't seen Davey around much lately. Is your brother training you to take over?"

Patronizing git.

"Might be. Did you want to talk to Davey?"

"Nah, nothing urgent. I'm selling my old Landcruiser ute, thought he might be interested."

"Why are you getting rid of it?"

"Got a new one on order, but the trade-in price they offered was a joke."

Two years into a drought and Gareth could afford a new Landcruiser? A ping of alertness had her glancing at Ryan, whose posture had stilled. He briefly raised and lowered his eyebrows, but Gareth missed it.

"I'll tell him you were asking after him, and if you don't hear from him, just give him a call. He's a bit busy, but he'll get back to you if you leave a message." The lie fell easily from her lips. "Another beer?"

Gareth shook his head and finished his drink.

"Nah, I'm driving. I heard you had new bar staff. I was hoping that meant new female talent as well as catching Davey for a chat." He tilted his head at Ryan. "No point hanging around today."

He slid off the stool and picked up his hat. "See ya another day, Aurora. Tell Davey to give us a call if he's interested." He ambled out the front door, a blast of hot dry air coming in as he left.

Ryan strolled closer. "Thoughts?"

It was unnerving how he could read her. "I was thinking that I never liked him, and I couldn't see why Davey let him in. Now I'm looking at everyone like they're a potential druggie or dealer."

Ryan nodded. "That's reasonable given the circumstances, possibly with cause in his case. I'll keep an eye out. And pubs and crowded public places are where deals happen. Do you have any security cameras?"

Aurora shook her head. "I suggested installing them when I got back here. There was money going missing. Davey said he needed to wait until after the festival when finances were stronger. I guess he had other reasons for letting it slide."

She swallowed the lump in her throat. It felt disloyal but she was starting to wonder if she knew her brother at all. "Did you know anything about Davey doing drugs? You were so close once. You must have seen something?"

Ryan spread his hands.

"I can't tell you anything, I'm sorry. Both of us were too

into sport back then. And neither of us had any money for drugs. Our contact has been limited the last few years. I wish I could tell you more." His eyes showed concern, but his face was shielded. He was holding back something. He had the same look when he was a teenager, poker faced and refusing to talk about his dad. If he didn't want to talk about something, he was a brick wall. If he knew more, he wasn't ready to tell her. It struck her what a huge gamble she'd taken letting him in. What did she really know about him? Ten years was a long time. Should she even trust him? Maybe he wasn't the person they thought they knew. First chance she got, she had to dig a little deeper. He was hiding something. That last thing she needed in her life right now was someone else with secrets to hide.

* * *

Aurora knew she was being a bitch, but she couldn't seem to stop. She'd farewelled her mother with a bright smile, but it was completely fake. Earlier she'd snapped at the teenage kitchen hand for spilling sauce as she refilled bottles and made her cry. And she'd just bitten the head off the truck driver who'd parked in her Mazda when she wanted to run out to inspect the temporary camp at the showground, like the showground was going somewhere and she couldn't wait for half an hour. She stomped back inside the cool dark hallway of Thirsty's to make a few more calls in the office while she waited, cursing the erratic mobile service.

It was Ryan's fault she was irritable. He was everywhere at work, either his scent in a room he'd just left, or in front of her, dragging her eyes to the way his jeans cupped his butt when he bent to move boxes of beer, or the creases in front highlighting his package and making her wonder. In four days, he'd even invaded her dreams. This morning she'd woken in a tangle of twisted sheets with an ache between her thighs, disappointed to find herself alone after a sexy dream involving water streaming off Ryan's naked torso as he stalked out of a waterhole and chased her naked self into its green depths, while white cockatoos wheeled and screeched overhead. She'd woken as he'd reached for her to the scream of her alarm, the morning light a cruel blow.

Stalking down the corridor, the sound of tables and chairs scraping on the hard floor drew her attention to the dining room. She walked in to find Thirsty's regular Johnno had abandoned sports betting and turned around on his bar stool, watching with a bemused expression as Ryan and Ant shuffled a jukebox to the side of the old dance floor.

She'd made a half dozen calls trying to track down a jukebox with no success. Where the hell had it come from?

"What's going on?" Impatience colored her voice, but she didn't care. She didn't have time for this. She needed to adjust the workflow schedule around a delay installing temporary fencing to establish the musician's camp. Ryan oversaw Thirsty's, for now, but the men had lists of tasks for the day. Clearing the dance floor and setting up a jukebox wasn't one of them. Good ideas were only good if they didn't jeopardize the timeline and they had barely enough staff to manage as it was.

Ryan looked up, a guilty expression on his face.

"It was going to be a surprise."

"Oh, I'm surprised all right." Aurora jerked her head at the door. "Ryan, can I speak with you please?"

She turned on her heel and left the room, ignoring Johnno's chuckles and Ant's look of confusion.

In the hallway she took a deep breath and held it in, then released it slowly, reminding herself to be positive and not nit-picky. She was the boss, she didn't need to justify or explain herself, but she did need to be fair. But it was hard to focus when Ryan arrived and was within touching distance, slouching against a wall, as relaxed as she was wired.

He crossed his arms, drawing attention to the width of his chest.

Her mouth went dry. The man was built. Her hands itched to find out if the muscles under that shirt were as hard as they looked. She shoved her fists in her pockets instead.

"Hey. Something I can do for you?" The way his lips were struggling not to curve up was petrol to her smoldering mood.

"Don't BS me, Ryan Harrington. What do you think you're doing?"

He chuckled and the urge to slap him was strong. What was it about this guy that always got under her skin? Cool calm Aurora, capable of wrestling a ten-page spreadsheet to the ground and negotiating with a hostile trade union rep without raising a sweat, brought undone by a chuckle.

"Chill, Aurora. I heard you'd been looking for a jukebox. I know a guy who knows a guy. It was supposed to be a surprise. I thought you'd like it. Come on, you do like it, don't you?"

And then he smiled at her, a proper smile, full of warmth and cheek and charm, for her eyes only, and it curled her toes and all the starch and irritation of the day faded. Because she was that girl again. And he was that guy.

When no one was watching, they'd shared moments like this, when he'd looked at her like making her smile was all he wanted to achieve in his day. Which was why when things had gone so horribly wrong that night, she really hadn't seen it coming.

She would be wise to remember that.

"I guess I should say thank you. Thank you, Ryan."

"I have another surprise, if you trust me."

Did she? Probably more than she should. Google had been disappointingly unhelpful, and Ryan wasn't on any social media she used. It was almost like he didn't exist. She'd even briefly wondered if he was a spy. Even though every echo from the past urged her to be careful, when he turned, she followed him back into the dining room.

*J*ohnno had gone back to watching the fourth race at Flemington on the sports television but mustn't have laid any bets because he twisted in his seat to observe them.

Ryan grabbed her hand and the shock of his touch made her want to snatch it away. His fingers were warm and firm as he led her towards to dance floor. "Let me convince you."

Johnno called out. "You can't knock back his idea without giving it a test-drive."

She yanked her hand away, turned, and glared.

"Who died and made you boss, Johnno? Or are you the Outback's answer to Fred Astaire? I don't have enough insurance to cover you if you put your back out dancing."

Johnno chuckled. "Sorry, Aurora. I'd ask you to dance, but I only dance with Maureen. She'd give me a black eye otherwise."

The opening bars to *The Time of My Life* sounded behind her and she whirled around.

Next to the old jukebox, Ryan had a half smile on his face. He held out a hand, did a little two-step shuffle, and shimmied his hips suggestively. He was playing it for laughs, but he failed. The man was sexy as sin.

Aurora shook her head. "Now you're not playing fair." *Dirty Dancing* was her other teenage obsession. He remembered.

Ryan said nothing, just lifted his chin in a challenge,

hooked his finger, and gestured for her to come closer, one boot tapping time to the beat, eyes focused on her.

Her heart rate kicked. *This was such a bad idea.* But she could no more resist than the tide could resist the moon. And he knew it. She surrendered and stepped onto the polished timber, anticipation skittering along her nerve endings.

Ryan's nostrils flared and he took her hand and stepped backward, pulling her along, eyes locked on hers, a cocky grin in place. If he felt the same tingle of awareness up his arm, he masked it, but she saw his eyes darken.

His scent, earthy and male, teased her nostrils, and the familiar pull of desire coiled in her belly. She suddenly didn't care that she was playing with fire, she felt alive and the stress hanging over her fell away. When he tugged her hand, she spun and circled into his arm, then whirled out again, in time with the music, joy in her limbs and laughter on her lips. They circled the dance floor in game of catch and release, light touches and finger-tips curling, her breath quickening, giggles escaping as her spirits soared with the music.

They'd never danced together before, but they moved easily, in tune with each other. As the song climbed, Aurora's senses buzzed, reacting to the reality of being in Ryan's arms, his attention wholly on her. The faded décor of the room disappeared.

When Ryan finally drew her body against his, beneath her palms she felt his heart beating as fast as hers. As she raised her eyes to his face, she couldn't look away.

Playful Ryan was gone. He knew what the song and the movie had meant to her, but did he know how much it meant to dance to it with him? Was the muscle ticking at his jaw a sign that he'd been as affected as her? *Maybe.* His breathing was uneven and his lips temptingly close. His hands tightened on her waist.

She could close the distance. She leaned …

Applause and a wolf whistle pierced the air and the moment shattered.

"Jump, Aurora, jump!" Johnno's chortle jarred like a bucket of water and she drew back.

"Go on, Ryan, do the big lift finale! She can't weigh that much!"

Aurora crashed back to earth. She was still tethered to Ryan, his hands at her waist as they moved apart. Something like regret flickered before his face became a mask.

It was the slap to the face she needed.

She'd learned nothing. Some traitorous inner recess of her heart was hooked on seeing what wasn't there where this man was concerned. She couldn't allow herself to forget that again. But pride wouldn't let her show her roiling emotions. Ryan's hands fell to his side as he released her, but the imprint of his steady grip burned her waist as he stepped away.

Johnno was still clapping, so Aurora fixed a small smile on her face as she turned and took a curtsy in his direction. As she rose, she glanced at Ryan and took a measure of comfort from the line of tension in his shoulders. Gathering her dignity, she walked away and threw her voice over her shoulder as she left.

"Alright. The dance floor stays, for now. But next bright idea, come and talk to me first okay, Ryan?"

"Sure thing, boss."

* * *

*R*yan had his guard up when he sought out Aurora later that day. He was still reeling from the fallout of his lapse of judgement. He'd forgotten how susceptible he was to Aurora. His simple plan to distract her and give her a reprieve from the pressure she was under for a few moments with some harmless fun had worked. But he'd miscalculated the risk. Now he knew how perfectly she fit in his arms.

He couldn't un-know that.

And when they shared that moment at the end of the dance, he realized she knew it too. If she called him on it, he wasn't confident he could deny her. And that would risk the only true relationships he'd ever had in his life, with her family. If he lost Davey and Rosemary, he really would become a husk of a man, just like his father.

He'd hurt her enough when he rejected her ten years ago. He'd known she'd had a crush on him. But he'd been blind-sided to find her naked in his bed, and then terrified that his dad would arrive home drunk any minute. There had been no thought, just reaction, throwing her clothes at her and bundling her out of the house. He couldn't have Aurora discover what his dad was really like, and he couldn't risk giving his dad something to hold over him. *God, what a mess.* He shook his head at the memory of his nineteen-year-old self. No wonder she was still prickly.

Entering the bar, Gwen was behind the counter, not Aurora. She was wearing her staff polo today, he noticed. Aurora must have had a win. Good for her. Gwen raised her brows in inquiry.

"You looking for the boss? She's in the office. Brace your-self, she's not having a great day."

"Thanks for the heads up. I can handle it."

"I've no doubt of that." She tilted her chin. "Just don't add to her woes, okay?"

"Excuse me?" His senses prickled at her tone.

Gwen was eyeing him steadily. How much did she know? Maybe Davey had confided in her about the loan? Aurora obviously didn't know, and he wasn't about to tell her. It was between him and Davey.

"If you're not planning on sticking around for the festival, let her know now."

Relief and irritation spiked, along with guilt. Gwen didn't know, that was good. But who the hell was she to question him? He wasn't about to leave Aurora in the lurch, but he had obligations.

"I don't plan on letting her down." His tone was curt, but Gwen didn't flinch.

"Good to know." She half smiled and turned back to restocking the fridge.

Ryan shook his head. He couldn't afford to waste any more time. He needed Aurora to relinquish the reins so he could manage Thirsty's but not drop the ball with preparations for publicly listing HLR Group on the stock exchange. The change from private to public company would turn him from a multi-millionaire into a paper billionaire, but more importantly, it would fund expansion and create thousands of jobs. He needed more time in the office to juggle his commitments. She either trusted him, or she didn't.

As he walked toward the office door, he heard her raised voice on the other side. He listened as Aurora talked to someone on the phone. He tensed. Back in the day, Aurora went off like a firecracker when provoked, much to Davey's delight. Right now, she was under so much pressure. How was she keeping it together? He listened, not catching the words, as she reigned in her frustrated tone. When he heard her put the phone down, he knocked and went in without waiting.

"Hey, Aurora. What's doing?" He leaned on the doorframe.

She chewed her lip, stress lines around her mouth.

"My contract labor hire firm has just bailed. Too hard to get people to come out here for two weeks' work, apparently." She dropped her head.

"What are you going to do?"

She sighed. "Grab a cup of coffee and start making calls. I have a backup firm, but I'd prefer not to use them. They're not experienced enough. Sydney's never felt so far away."

He felt a surge of respect. One challenge after another and she didn't shy away, even when she must be worried sick. She was a fighter. But this was an opportunity he couldn't waste.

"I can help. Let me make a few calls. I've got some contacts and a few people owe me some favors at work."

"Where do you work again?" She looked wary. It shouldn't burn, but it did. Did she not trust him? Or just not like him? Or did she remember his father and wonder how much of that man was in him? A sour taste filled his mouth. Self-doubt only shadowed him in this town.

"HLR Group. They're in hospitality." He was owner and chairman of the board, currently AWOL in the Outback. With his company's stock exchange launch due in less than a month, his absence might spook investors. He couldn't let down the team working on this. The less he shared with anyone, including Aurora, the better.

"I've heard of them. Big business. I tried googling you, you know. You're invisible online. That doesn't happen by accident."

"You googled me?" He tilted his chin down and grinned.

"Of course. First rule of human resource management. That's all." Aurora squirmed in her seat.

He quelled his smile.

"What have you been doing for the past ten years?" she said, her brow crinkling.

He waved away her question.

"We can catch up another time," he lied. "I'd better make those calls now. How many days have you got before you need people on site?" Keeping his private life private was a habit. People treated you differently when they thought you were successful, just like when they thought you were trash. That's why his media team spent more time erasing his profile than creating it. It was better to be the gray man. It worked in his favor. People underestimated him all the time in negotiations. Usually only once.

"Ten days. Don't remind me." She stifled a yawn. "Use my office. I need coffee and a break." She grabbed her handbag and slung it over her shoulder. "I'll be back in an hour. If you have no luck by then I'll need to phone my second choice. The clock is ticking. Thanks, Ryan."

"Thank me when you get back and I've got a solution in place."

She crossed her fingers. "It's my biggest headache. I'd give anything for a quick result."

His felt his lips curl up at the corners and suppressed a grin as she realized what she'd said and rolled her eyes.

"Well, almost anything." Aurora closed the door behind her as she left.

He laughed and picked up the phone. Teasing Aurora almost made it worthwhile being back in Granite Ridge. Almost …

CHAPTER 5

$\mathcal{R}$yan took advantage of the office time to quickly respond to pressing emails and then phoned Tracey to outline his plan to help Aurora and how best to implement it. And as expected, she called him back within minutes to say his chief problem solver was on the job and would have a team on the road by the end of the week. Sometimes it really was fun being the big boss.

Aurora took some convincing. But eventually, after a phone call from the head of the specialist crisis management field relief team, she was persuaded.

"I don't know how you pulled that off, Ryan, but I really appreciate it. If Davey calls, it will be great to have some good news to share." She chewed her lip. Anxiety about her brother must be eating her alive. If it had been anyone else, he might have given them a hug. Since that moment on the dancefloor, he couldn't risk touching her. Instead he pressed his advantage.

"He knows you can handle this, Aurora. But I agree, anything that helps him focus on doing what he needs to do to get well, must be a bonus. Are you ready to let me handle the day to day management at Thirsty's until your job with the festival is done?"

Her desktop and the bottom of her computer screen were papered with a grid of sticky notes, and she had a small pile where one item after another was being added as she crossed it off her list. Sunlight streamed in through the blind slats as the sun drew closer to the hilltop ridge outside town. She looked tired, her fingers already moving the computer mouse and scrolling through an open spreadsheet.

"I guess it makes sense. You already know the stock control system and the software Davey uses. But any questions, make sure you come to me, okay?"

"Of course. It's your family business. Listen, you look like you need a break. My old footy coach Des is coming in to say gidday in a bit. He's going to prep the clubhouse facilities for the incoming workers. You should come down and say hi."

She looked up, harried, but nodded. "Okay, sure."

A while later, Ryan pushed a frothy beer glass across the counter to the man who'd coached him since Under Eights, about life as much as about rugby. "Your money's no good here today. I reckon I owe you more than a few beers for all you did for me." He pulled a note from his wallet and rang up the sale, putting his cash in the till.

Des accepted the gesture, raised his glass in a toast, and winked. "Here's to the prodigal son returning."

Ryan tilted his head. "Cheers, but this is only temporary. My rugby days are well behind me." *And I am no one's prodigal son.*

"I always knew you'd come back."

Ryan just smiled. "So, how are the mighty Crushers?"

"Having a bit of a dry spell. We haven't made it to a grand final the past two seasons. Haven't won one in six years. It's not too late for you to pull on the jersey, half the team are over thirty. You're only twenty-nine, aren't you? Practically a pup. Pre-season training starts in a month. It's a shame Davey's injury put him out for good, it would have been magic to get the old team back together." His crinkly eyes were hopeful.

Ryan felt an unexpected twinge of nostalgia. They'd had some good times, particularly the away trips. "Anyone left around town that I'd remember?"

The older man scratched his head. He'd aged a lot, but ten years in the sun working on the council's road repair crew could do that.

"Look, to be honest, we've lost too many. It used to be to better jobs away in the mines." He shook his head, his face sad and a little bewildered. "These days, it's suicide and drugs. It's not easy."

Des's words felt like a rugby boot to the face. The only escape option he'd considered was leaving town. He'd never considered he might have gotten away lightly.

"That's terrible. I'm so sorry to hear that."

Des waved his reply away. "Well, it is what it is. Tough times for a lot of people, and the drought doesn't help. Let's talk about something more cheerful. How's Aurora?"

"I'm just fine. Ryan looking after you?" She slid onto a bar stool next to her brother's old coach, leaned across and kissed his grizzled cheek, her expression fond. Ryan felt like an outsider. She'd gone back to being formal and stiff with him since the jukebox incident. But maybe it was for the best. He didn't want her to look at him with affection. He was here to pay back a debt to her family, buy Davey time to get his shit together, and then get back to his real life. Des chuckled and glanced between the two of them, his expression scheming.

"He sure is, love. It's his shout. What would you like to drink?"

Aurora laughed, her eyes sparkling. Reaction hit him in

the solar plexus. He hadn't seen her relax like this since he got here. He grabbed a chilled white wine glass and a bottle of New Zealand sauvignon blanc, holding it up for her approval. She smiled.

"Well, since you put it like that, and that's my favorite wine, how can I refuse? Thanks, Ryan."

He passed it to her and their fingers touched, reaction to her skin hitting him again. She glanced at his face, then away quickly, and he knew she felt something too.

Des sipped his beer thoughtfully. "Have you had a chance to check out the changes around town?"

"Not yet."

"Well, make sure you show him around, Aurora. There've been a few improvements, and some things have gone backwards, I'll admit. But it's always good to know what's going on."

He stared pointedly at Ryan. "We need people to care about this place, otherwise it will die. We need investment. Locals can only do so much; we need out-of-town folk to get involved. Besides, former residents can help the city folk to understand why they should visit, don't you reckon, Aurora?"

She glanced at him with a look of apology.

"I think Ryan's doing enough already."

Her shielding made him feel worse. Guilt tightened his chest, but Des wasn't finished. He pointed a meaty finger at Ryan.

"Ryan needs to see for himself what's happened to the town. It's going to be all fun times, fireworks, and music for the festival, but after that's done, no disrespect, Aurora, things go back to normal. For a lot of people, that's not a great place." He stopped abruptly, as though he'd seen Ryan's father, a ghost at the end of the bar. "You don't need me telling you that. But look around anyway."

He owed Des. He'd been a tough coach, but his coaching style was 'if it's not positive, it's pointless'. He'd known more about Ryan's home life than most and made sure Ryan knew he could talk to him. Thanks to Des, rugby was a safe and supportive place to hang out. He'd also pushed him hard to be the best he could be on and off the field and found a way to make sure Ryan's fees were paid so he could play. Des knew him and he knew the older man was right. Much as he'd intended to avoid it, the past was around every corner. But he could handle it.

"Okay, Des, I will." He turned to Aurora. "Actually, Aurora, can you show me around later? It shouldn't take long. Unless you're scared of motorbikes?"

Des chortled.

Aurora rolled her eyes. "Is that your idea of a dare? I'm happy to show you around when you finish your shift. That's if you can find me a helmet."

Ryan met her look of challenge with one of his own.

"No problem. I'll meet you outside at six."

* * *

Waiting outside later, Aurora didn't know why she'd agreed to this. A sensible alternative would be to insist on driving her little Mazda, but some devil inside insisted she torment herself by wrapping her arms around Ryan's muscled torso and sliding her legs snugly around his thighs while a powerful black motorcycle throbbed beneath her. She was unlikely to ever have the chance again, she reasoned.

Then he sauntered out the staff door, two black helmets in hand, all dark and dangerous, and the lies she'd told herself about being unaffected by Ryan fell away.

Her mouth dried. This was bad. *Very bad.*

Her eyes drank him in and she swallowed, her mouth suddenly moist. Drool would definitely give her away.

Midnight hair, dark stubbled jaw, worn black leather jacket, faded jeans that hugged his thighs indecently, and black boots coated in dust from the open road. Then he hit her with that laid-back grin. He was in his element. She was so far out of hers, she wanted to whimper, instead of standing mesmerized, forgetting how to breathe.

He handed her one of the helmets and then looked her up and down, gaze lingering.

It was late, but sunset was still an hour away. The air was still hot and dry, the smell of the warm bitumen and dust in her nostrils. She shifted from foot to foot and fiddled with her sunglasses, then stopped herself, blowing out a slow, deep, self-calming breath.

"You won't need sunglasses; the visor is tinted. I'll stow them for you. Good to see you wore jeans and boots. Sensible girl."

Sensible girl? Her spirits flagged. Was that how Ryan saw her?

He shrugged out of his jacket and handed it to her.

"I'll keep to a safe speed, but my hide is tough. Wear this. That long sleeve shirt is probably fine, unless you're planning to take me to the lookout to watch the moon rise, in which case, maybe something skimpier?" He raised his eyebrows devilishly and she shook her head at him, reminding herself it was just banter and to ignore the stupid jump of her heart.

"No? Ah well, a man can dream." His grin was obscured as he slid on his helmet.

She thrust her arms into his jacket. The weight of it and his scent immediately enveloped her and her skin prickled in reaction, nipples tightening as though he'd traced a finger along her naked spine. Flustered, she tried to sound unaffected, but the higher pitch of her voice gave her away.

"If you're going to be a pest, you can find someone else to give you the grand tour. I've got plenty of other things I could be doing."

He laughed as he inserted a key into the motorbike's ignition, turning it, then revving the engine. He cupped his hand against his helmet near where his ear would be, pretending he hadn't heard her, his expression mischievous. But when he swung a leg over the machine and straddled it, he grabbed her hand and tugged her closer, and damn if she didn't lean in, helpless against gravity and the pull of attraction, her heart doing that flip flop thing that drove her crazy. He took the helmet from her hand and loosened the chin strap with nimble fingers, then reached up and smoothed her curls behind her ears. It was all she could do not to tremble. Lust and adrenaline were spiking already, and he'd barely scraped her skin.

"When you put this on, you'll want to pull the straps wide to create space in the padding for it to glide over your ears comfortably, okay? I'll help you do it up. And I'm not miked up, so we won't be able to chat in between stops. Have you ridden a bike much?"

She shook her head, too off kilter by the close proximity to pretend cool reserve. "Never," she managed to choke. He smelled of warm skin and hot male. She was only human. Snuggling up against his back was going to be exquisite torture.

"You'll be safe with me. Follow my lead. Lean the way I lean and if you don't feel comfortable, close your eyes, and hang on, I'll do the leaning for both of us. We'll take a little spin and then I'll stop and see how you're going. Are you sure you're up for this?" His gaze was serious.

She knew he'd let her cut her losses and retain her dignity if she wanted to bail. No wonder she'd hero worshipped him once. But that wasn't going to happen. He had been amazing helping her out. She wouldn't have been mortal not to be moved. Besides, she owed it to her teenage self to climb aboard his black beast and grab on to Ryan with both hands just for the thrill.

"Let's do this," she said.

"Okay." He helped her fasten the helmet, his hands gentle under her chin, and pointed out where she would be resting her feet, and the bar she could hold on to for stability behind her if she preferred. It seemed horribly vulnerable and her nerves spiked.

"Hop on."

He slid forward to create space for her behind him. Aurora gulped, braced one hand on his shoulder, took strength from the solidness there, and gathered her courage. She launched her foot over the seat and hopped and slid awkwardly into place, trying to keep some space between them and wriggling back on the leather seat.

She had no time to dwell on the risk she was taking putting her life and her yearning heart in Ryan's care before he grabbed her hand and wrapped it around his waist. He brushed her fingers over his muscles and pressed them against his torso with a squeeze. She stifled a gasp and it was all she could do not to dig her fingers into his warm flesh. And then he reached around behind her and pushed her forward until she was meshed against his back. This time she did gasp. The intimacy sent a flare of heat deep in her belly.

She could feel the rumble of his laughter. And with a roar of the engine, they peeled off out of the carpark.

CHAPTER 6

*B*uying the bike had been one of Ryan's best decisions. He could easily have afforded something custom and showy, but that wasn't his style. Its specs were hidden—high performance masked by a muscular matte-black exterior. But it had never given him more joy than today, revisiting the town he'd left behind, with Aurora's hot body wrapped around him, holding tight like she never wanted to let go.

Ryan was hyper-aware of her every movement, her little gasp and the tightening of her fingers on his hips as they leaned into the first corner. At first, she didn't react as they slowed for a bend, but soon she was leaning like a pro, attuned to his body language in a way that made a primal part of his brain roar.

Twenty minutes later, he pulled into the Crusher's home-field carpark and stopped, cutting the engine and lowering the kick stand. Aurora slid off the seat behind him and gave an awkward little hop as she pulled her leg over, one hand on his shoulder for balance, reminding him how petite she was. She had such a fierce personality, he tended to forget that. He liked her leaning on him. Her presence on the bike, laminated to his back as they took corners, aroused other feelings entirely. He shifted on the seat and pulled off his helmet, running his fingers through his hair. Keeping his hands off his best friend's sister was becoming increasingly challenging, especially if he read her interest and efforts at self-restraint correctly.

"How are you travelling so far?"

Her helmet muffled her reply. She was trying to undo the chin strap and failing, so he beckoned her over, tipping up her visor.

"You can leave it on, we won't be here long." Her eyes were bright with excitement and she smiled at him. He liked every way she looked at him, even annoyed, but smiling and happy was becoming addictive. He ignored the internal warning alarm that thought set off. Making things right with Aurora was not his purpose in being here.

"This is fun. It's a great feeling to have the air rushing over you. I can see the attraction. It's very freeing."

Her enjoyment made him happy. On the road, he was just a man, hidden behind the visor. No expectations, nothing to prove, the open road offering a reprieve from the endless striving at new goals, hoping to fill the void inside. He came closest to contentment when the road ahead stretched empty to the horizon. It pleased him more than he wanted to acknowledge that she got it.

Aurora squinted into the sun sinking lower in the sky and looked around the dusty dead grass of the playing field. Ryan judged they had an hour before it sank below the trees edging the field in the west.

"Are you reliving your glory days?"

Ryan laughed. "Nah. It meant a lot at the time and I still love rugby, but now I'm happy to watch other people put their bodies on the line."

"Did you play anywhere else after you left here?"

Ryan shook his head.

"I would have liked to, but I couldn't commit to a team because I was working shifts." He'd worked his butt off at the hotel that gave him his first break. His boss and mentor promptly put him in charge of his own hotel. He'd never looked back, only forward. "Too much training anyway."

Aurora smiled and placed a hand on his bicep. "Looks to me like you're still working out."

He stilled.

She left her fingers wrapped around his muscle and his eyes met hers, huge inside the visor. She half-smiled at him and her teeth nibbled her lush bottom lip.

An urge to sweep his tongue over the same path was strong, especially when her lips parted, and the pink tip of her tongue emerged to soothe the bitten skin. He swallowed a groan. Ignoring their attraction wasn't working, especially when she looked at him like he was a tempting treat she longed to taste. They weren't teenagers anymore.

"Aurora…"

"Hmmm?"

"I like it when you touch me." His voice was rough.

Her half-smile amped up to wicked then, and he was a goner.

It was all the response he needed. He flipped down her visor.

"Hop back on. I've got some places to see." He pulled on his helmet and slid forward on the seat so she could slide back on, firing the motorbike's engine. His was already warm.

* * *

57

*a*urora was surprised when Ryan sped up as they passed their old high school, rather than slow down. Then again, his memories of school probably weren't as good as hers, she recalled. There had been a break-in and Ryan had been number one suspect, until police found stolen printers and computers elsewhere. God, how had she forgotten that? No wonder he'd left town and not come back. It had been completely unfair. Yet he'd been nothing but stoic. But that kind of shame and anger left scars. Being raised in a single parent family, she'd had her share of scorn thrown at her by people who didn't know her father had died when she was so young she knew nothing different. Her mother and brother had been annoyingly overprotective, but they'd lived comfortably because of a life insurance pay-out. Ryan's situation was different. No one knew anything about his mother, just that she had 'shot through' years ago. And his dad was rarely seen except disappearing into or getting thrown out of the town's three pubs. Ryan never talked about him and they'd rarely been inside his house. She wondered if they'd stop at the cemetery.

No. The bike rumbled on, its vibrations travelling to places on her body that were already over stimulated, not that she minded, at all. They rode past the council chambers and the new YMCA, but still Ryan didn't stop. He'd avoided his old house, now deserted, down by the abandoned railway yards. All pretense of a tour apparently now abandoned, Aurora tried not to read too much into it and instead surrendered to the thrill of being meshed against the man her body insisted on craving. Emboldened by his admission and the desire she'd read in his eyes earlier, she slid her fingers under his shirt, stifling a groan as she felt his warm muscles tense under her palms.

The road surface beneath them changed as the bike

turned from the bitumen onto a gravel road ridged with corrugations that added to the tension thrumming in her. The winding road was one she'd never visited. It led away from town and narrowed until it ended at a gated fire trail. A small sign insisted the track was for 'authorized personnel only'. But Ryan turned off the engine and stood, powerful thighs holding the bike in place, flipping his visor.

"We're here for a bit. You can take off your helmet." There was a trace of strain in his deep voice, like he was imagining her taking off more than the safety gear.

She slid off the bike and grabbed onto his arm for support, and he grabbed her arm too, strong fingers curling around her forearm, the contact spiking a ridiculous thrill.

"You okay?" His voice was gruff.

Aurora nodded and released him as she found her footing. She'd been wired before the ride; if he touched her again, she'd probably implode. Exhaling slowly, she fumbled with the chin strap, willing her heartbeat to slow, the heavy helmet suddenly claustrophobic.

Ryan kicked down the stand, stepped off the bike, and removed his helmet, setting it on the mirror with relaxed fluid movements. His mouth curved slightly, his gaze watchful.

She felt so edgy she couldn't do simple tasks, fumbling and failing to release the buckle.

He waited a beat then reached over and steadied her shoulders, his touch like electricity sparking her nerve endings.

He flipped up her visor and smiled at her. "Easy there, let me help. There's a knack to it."

She was torn between pulling away or leaping into his arms. Instead she slanted her head so he could work at the buckle and release it, breathing in his scent. Finally, the helmet was off and she stepped back, turning away and fluffing her curls with her fingers, hiding the flush she could feel on her face. She pretended interest in the bushland surrounds and shed his leather jacket, draping it over the bike seat.

"I've never been here, isn't that weird? What's the reason for the track and the path?" Her voice sounded strained.

"It's a fire trail they keep clear for the rural fire brigade as an access point for the hill. You can't ride trail bikes here, though I think occasional bushwalkers used to use it." Ryan's voice was behind her, but he wasn't looking at her. He had opened one of the bike's black leather saddle bags and was moving things around, tucking the jacket inside.

Aurora turned as Ryan settled a small backpack onto his broad shoulders.

"Are you okay with a short walk?"

She nodded. After their moment in the Crushers car park, they'd crossed some threshold, but he'd become quiet again. The chance to settle her nerves appealed. They set off up the trail, dry leaves crunching underfoot and sunlight dappling the tree roots and rocks. The scent of the eucalyptus trees and low scrubby brush filled her nose and she took a moment to enjoy the contrast to Thirsty's where she barely noticed the smell of beer now. She caught a waft of lemon myrtle and a sweet aroma from flowering gums. It made her sigh and her muscles loosened a little, enjoying the slight uphill walk. The days were long this time of year, so they still had a while before darkness.

The trail switched back and forth and rose slowly, and Ryan reached out a hand to her to help her over a fallen log. "Nearly there." He didn't let go of her hand and instead lead her off the path on a narrower track, so narrow only kangaroos or wallabies might use it. There was a granite boulder ahead and the track appeared to edge around it. "Close your eyes for the last bit."

"Seriously, isn't that dangerous?"

"Don't you trust me?"

She laughed. "Probably more than I should."

He squeezed her hand. His hooded gaze sent heat flushing to her cheeks. He looked like he wanted to devour her. She felt like she wanted to let him. The sense of impending change was heavy in the air. She closed her eyes and surrendered. He tugged her hand and she followed. She brushed against the boulder and felt longer grass against her legs, grateful for her boots as security against hidden snakes. She followed Ryan blindly, his hand reassuring as he drew her along behind him. Light dappled through her eyelids, flashing pink.

"Okay, open them."

She did and blinked, stunned at the vista.

"Oh, Ryan! It's beautiful …" A smile curved her lips. They were halfway up one of the smaller hills that circled the town. A soft breeze lifted her curls in a lemon myrtle-scented caress. They stood in an open semicircle beyond the tree line where knee-high grass rippled in the breeze. They were on one of the "balds" she'd read about in the Granite Ridge newspaper she realized, and a surge of appreciation swelled. Elders from the town's Aboriginal community had the town council's support to manage the burning that kept the balds healthy and grasses and wildlife in balance with the surrounding forest. Pinks and purples were starting to tint the sky, and beyond the trees they were high enough to have a clear view of the township spreading on the plain below.

"How did you know this spot was here?"

He smiled at her, but his face was tinged with banked emotion too.

"I found it when I was about ten and I came here pretty often. Camped out a few times."

"Did Davey come here?"

61

"No, just me. I've never shown anyone else. It was just somewhere to hide out when I needed to. It was a good place to think. Or not to think …"

He went quiet, his gaze fixed on the horizon, but she knew he wasn't sight-seeing; he was thinking about being ten and having the kind of life a child shouldn't have to run away from.

She wished he didn't have that haunted look on his face.

The breeze picked up, warm air caressing her skin.

Ryan stood with his hands on his hips, gazing at the scene. He glanced at her and she was struck by yearning so hard she couldn't breathe. Her heart whumped in her chest.

"What?"

"Just admiring the view."

She stared at his familiar face in the softening golden light and bit her lip against the slow burn of desire thickening her blood. Did he feel it too? She stepped forward, into his personal space.

His gaze darkened and the corner of his mouth lifted. "Aurora …"

"Hmmm?"

"You're playing with fire, Red."

She smiled. "I like danger. Now kiss me, Ryan Harrington, or get the hell out of my bar and my life."

One side of his mouth quirked at that, just a little, and the energy sparking between them changed from restraint to anticipation. His eyes mirrored the challenge in hers. "Yes, boss," he murmured, and his mouth descended.

Aurora's eyes fluttered closed and her lips were still smiling as her mouth met his. But when Ryan's lips settled gently over hers, the sounds of the bush, the sunset, the scenery, the smells, all fell away. There was only the contact, his lips first brush against hers, his arms reaching to encircle her, the thump of the heartbeat in his chest and the answering clamor in her own.

His lips ignited something that had simmered so long she'd forgotten its potential.

Because light and tender burned out within seconds of contact, turned into moist mouths parting and meeting with a hunger to know and to cherish and to claim. Fire scorched through Aurora's veins, across her skin. She heard him make a sound of capitulation, felt it reverberate through his chest as he hauled her closer, the hardness pressing into her belly telling her she wasn't alone in the storm of need his lips were unleashing. Her hands grabbed fistfuls of his shirt and his arms wrapped tight around her as her knees faltered. This was not a kiss, this was a chemical chain reaction, and nothing could ever be the same again. When they broke apart, panting and dazed, Aurora looked to the ground expecting to see scorched earth.

* * *

*R*yan pulled away, but it was already too late. Blood pounded in his ears while every cell in his body screamed at him to kiss her again, taste her and touch her and make her lose her mind with need, kiss her until she couldn't remember her own name.

It was supposed to be a simple kiss. But the look on Aurora's face slammed the door hard on the idea that this could be as easy as two adults taking a moment to answer a forgotten question, nothing big at stake. She wore every emotion she was feeling right there on her face, from the look of wonder to the slight puffiness and sheen of moisture on her lips.

She raised her eyes to his, a shy smile as she touched her

fingertips to her plumped lips. She looked so damn … smug??? It made him nervous.

"Aurora …" Ryan ran his fingers through his hair. "I can't offer you anything."

Her expression lost a little of its sparkle, but she shook her head.

"Getting ahead of yourself much? Who says I need anything from you? We're adults here. You're not seeing someone, are you?"

He shook his head.

"Me either. Don't tell me you're scared, Harrington?"

Terrified would be closer to the truth. She touched places in him he preferred buried. He placed his hand over hers and growled, "This isn't a rope swing dare. If you want this, there can't be any expectations. And it has to be off grid." He wasn't staying and he didn't want the Granite Ridge rumor mill focused on him and creating expectations he couldn't meet. Or his off-grid location finding its way to public attention at such a crucial time for his business.

"Your bad-boy reputation is safe with me, Ryan." She moistened her lips with the tip of her tongue. "And I can play by your rules. There will be playing, won't there?"

Emotion winded him like a bare-knuckled fist to belly. Her face was an open book. He read desire there, and more terrifying, trust. She trusted him not to hurt her, that they could both walk away unscathed. That was more than he could guarantee. But he'd make damn sure that they had a good time exploring this crazy chemistry before it ended, as it inevitably would. You had to have a heart to give, and his was so scarred it wasn't worth offering.

Her phone rang, the sound jarring. She winced and fished it out of her back pocket. "Sorry, I've got to take this."

He watched her face, noting the flush of arousal on her

skin. She sighed, frown lines reappearing. "Ant, what's up?" Her eyes widened. "I'm on my way." She ended the call.

"There's a problem. We have to go. Playtime will have to wait." She turned and started walking back to the bike. He followed, uncertain whether he was disappointed or relieved.

CHAPTER 7

$\mathcal{R}$yan spotted a winding trail of vehicles clogging the main street and slowed the bike as they neared Thirsty's. Aurora hadn't exaggerated. Definitely a problem. There were dozens of caravans and four-wheel-drives and campervans, way more than the town was ready to handle at short notice, he guessed.

The convoy wrapped around the block, right up to the locked entry gate to the temporary caravan park behind the pub. The fenced site was being prepped to accommodate a dozen bands and their crews, due to arrive within days to set up for the Muster in the Dust music festival. A police car was parked next to the gates and the pot-bellied sergeant was standing talking to several men and women clustered in a small group. One of the men was waving his arm at the vacant lot.

The hotel's rear driveway was blocked with traffic, so he was forced to cruise past and into the main street to park in a space right out the front.

Aurora slid off the bike and unbuckled his spare helmet, her movements quick as she handed it to him. She fluffed her hair with her fingers. "I'd better get inside and see what's going on."

He put a hand on her forearm. "Do you want me to sort this out?"

She squinted at him in confusion and he inwardly cursed his mistake. He was so used to being the one who came up with the solutions at HLR Group. But she didn't know that. And this was Red—she didn't need rescuing.

"Why? It's not your problem." Perhaps realizing how blunt she sounded, she added, "Thanks, but it's nothing I can't manage, and you've done enough already. I'll call you later." And with that she spun on her heel and headed into Thirsty's.

When he finished securing the bike and followed, he had to push through a crowd to get behind the bar. Snagging an apron from the pile under the counter, he caught the tail end of the explanation Gwen offered Aurora.

"They just kept coming," she muttered. "They said the caravan park was full, so the van park sent them here to see if you'd open the musician's campground. They parked up and came in here to wait for an answer. It's chaos. I've called everyone I can get to come in and help and sent the customers to wait out the back in the beer garden. The kitchen is going off like a frog in a sock. Betty's granddaughters are helping..."

Aurora lifted a hand to stem the flow.

"You did exactly the right thing," she soothed, and Gwen's face relaxed, her shoulders lowering.

"Thanks. I just imagined what you would do, you always seem to know how to handle things. I'm so glad you're here now! And you too, Ryan. I'd better get these jugs of beer out there though." She hustled away.

Aurora glanced at Ryan, about to speak, but he preempted her question. "I'll take over here while you go do your thing, sorting out the travelers."

Aurora shot him a grateful smile and ducked into her office. She emerged wearing one of her Manager polo shirts and grabbed a jug of water and some glasses before heading out to the beer garden.

Ryan began pouring schooners of beer and taking shouted orders as fast as cash and cards could fly, then assigning jobs for the available staff as they arrived.

An hour later Johnno elbowed his way to the front of the bar and pretended to be gasping of thirst. "Christ on a bike! Have you seen the mob out there? It's like a Baby Boomer convention. Or maybe a flock of galahs. I've never seen so many gray heads in one location. Lucky Aurora's got them eating out of the palm of her hand," he said. "One more schooner and then I'm out of here."

After Ryan filled the order, he intercepted Gwen so he could deliver the next round of jugs to the beer garden himself and check what support Aurora needed. When he caught sight of her, he hesitated.

She was in her element. Her head was thrown back in laughter as she stood next to a table of mature men and women, who were laughing too. She stood out like a beacon with her shiny red curls and her youth and vivacity. Somehow it rammed the truth home. Aurora belonged here. He didn't. He was here under false pretenses. Acid clawed at his stomach.

It wasn't too late to back out of his deal with Aurora. She'd be pissed off, but she'd keep it to herself for her family's sake. She was as protective of them as he was. With events ramping up early, he could keep out of her way until he got a team in place and leave before he did anything he might regret. And finding out if their chemistry was as potent as he feared could be a huge mistake. He had no place in his life for complications and Aurora deserved better than that.

A booming male voice to his left caught his attention. An older man held up a scarred meaty hand the size of dinner plate and waved. The table was surrounded by a group of travelers, some eating, some finished; all were relaxed and enjoying themselves. One woman with bright red glasses and short white hair was showing her phone to another customer in a voluminous flowered dress who was swiping slowly, cooing at photos. A bald man was trying to coax a small white dog to stay hidden under his chair.

This crowd was exactly what he'd designed his first chain of hotels to attract. The venture had been so successful he'd replicated it around the country, specializing in turning ailing hotels into profitable ones and building custom venues that became destinations themselves in unique or picturesque locations. He should have felt right at home. But tonight, he felt like a fraud, a trespasser who would never belong.

"Over here, son."

The word—son—was a knife.

Parent was more like it. His father would never have been part of a scene like this. He'd have been long gone. He'd have started early in the day nursing small beer after small beer until he started slurring his words and bar staff refused to serve him, then he'd continue drinking at home, alone, until he passed out in front of the television, surrounded by empty brown bottles.

Shutting down the memory, Ryan placed the beers on the table and began collecting empty glasses. "How's everyone tonight?"

"Great, thanks," the unofficial spokesman answered, and cleared space for the jugs. "This is a cracking little town. Is this your pub? Enquiring minds would like to know." He leaned back in his chair, his belly still reaching the table, while his tiny wife tried to shush him with an elbow to the ribs.

"Reg, don't be so nosy."

Reg just laughed and put his hand over hers on his thigh, leaving it there. "He doesn't mind, love. Do ya mate?"

Ryan judged Reg was no threat to the peace, despite the red flush to his cheeks and his loud chattiness.

"Not at all. And it is a great little town. I'm just passing through. That woman over there, it's her place." He nodded at Aurora, who glanced over, caught him looking, and gave him a look with a hint of promise. He turned his head to the couple.

Reg chuckled. "I wouldn't be in a hurry to move on if I were you. She's a cracker, too!"

His wife swatted him with her free hand and Reg pretended to swerve.

"Now, Vera, you know I can pick a good sort a mile away, because I picked you." He tapped the side of his nose. "When you catch the interest of someone who looks at you like that, grab her with both hands and never let go. You won't regret it."

Vera clucked. "Okay, Reg, that's your limit. You get so sentimental when you've had too many beers! Sorry, love." She smiled at her husband fondly, and then rolled her eyes at Ryan.

He managed a tight smile. He wasn't seeking the kind of connection the older couple had. It had never been on his radar.

"No offence taken. You're husband's a very wise man. Reg, Vera." He nodded. "Enjoy your night."

A couple of hours later, Aurora met him on his way back to the bar with a load of empty glasses and let her arm brush against his as they went through the doorway together. It was casual, but not casual, a declaration of intent. Whatever his head said about getting out before things got messy, his body had other ideas, anticipation sending heat rippling in waves, just from the fleeting caress of the soft skin on her arm. God knew what would have happened if she'd grabbed him where he wanted.

He needed to end this, fast.

She shimmied ahead of him, stepping quickly, buzzing with energy fired by the night's events. "Phew, what a crowd! Good for business. I've sorted out a solution for tonight and tomorrow the mayor's arranged early access to the show-ground so they can use the amenities." She chattered on, oblivious to his tension. "Lucky Jazzy Parker is a friend. Thanks for staying on to help, Ryan. You seem to be making a habit of coming to my rescue. I'm thinking of ways of showing my gratitude." Her hum of appreciation was almost a growl as she gazed up at him with hungry eyes.

His blood heated another notch despite his resolve. He swallowed hard and glanced around to see if her comment had been overheard. "I thought we agreed on subtlety?"

Aurora just snorted. "I'm not the one who dropped me to the front door on the back of a noisy black motorbike. But I'll play your game. What do you suggest?"

Oh God. Aurora kept looking at him like he was a juicy steak and she was a starving woman. She'd hate him for what he was about to do, and he hated himself.

"Meet me in the kitchen in twenty."

CHAPTER 8

The kitchen was empty, but meals were waiting for them. Aurora was ravenous, so he put off his plan while they ate. Aurora backed out of the pantry, hands filled with cutlery and condiments. She dropped them to the table and slid into her seat, then picked up the tomato sauce bottle and proceeded to pour a precise swirl next to her pile of thick-cut chips, then neatly aligned them so they faced the same direction.

"You can take medication for that you know."

She looked up, frowning in confusion, so he pointed his chip at her tidy plate. She rolled her eyes.

"I don't remember you being so funny."

"Only around you."

That much was true. Tracey's eyes would be bulging to see him so unwound. Despite the constant tug of war over his attraction to the woman sitting opposite, since he'd arrived in Granite Ridge, he'd become almost ... relaxed. His executive assistant only knew the ice-cool business operator, always thinking three steps ahead. If only that detachment worked with Aurora. Instead of breaking things off before they went any further, like he intended, he was contemplating the seduction potential of the pub's kitchen table, his groin swelling in anticipation as he watched the way she licked the salt from her lips. She was driving him crazy.

"Thanks for backing me up tonight. We couldn't have managed without you. That's just a taste of what's coming next week, in case you want to split." She spoke lightly, but she fidgeted with the sauce bottle, twisting the lid open and closed. She caught him watching and stopped, putting the container down carefully, and lifted her chin in challenge.

Maybe she was picking up on his vibes and his uncertainty. She'd given him the perfect opening. All he had to do was take it. Admit he'd made a mistake.

Or was afraid of making one.

He stilled. Was that his problem? Fear? This was Aurora. She'd had no problem asking him for what she wanted. Him. No strings. That took guts, especially after their shared past.

The least he could do was be honest and admit he wanted her too, despite the fact it might be hard to walk away. He'd been honest—well, mostly honest—about his situation. If he gave them both what they wanted, where was the harm? He looked up and realized she was waiting on his answer.

"Not going to happen. You can quit worrying about me." He swirled a chip in his sauce then bit it in half, savoring the taste, salty and a little tart.

Her shoulders loosened a bit. "Sorry. I should be more gracious. I'm just not used to asking for help."

He grunted. "Eat. You'll need your strength."

She widened her eyes in mock surprise.

"Getting ahead of yourself much?"

He choked on his chip. He'd been thinking of the week ahead, not the night.

She laughed. "See, I can be funny too."

He shook his head and took a sip of water. "True, but I admire your other qualities."

She tilted her head. "I'm not sure I'm ready to hear what you think my best qualities are."

He read a note a vulnerability in her voice, regretted that he might have put it there by his lack of finesse years ago, when he'd had no option to act on his attraction.

"You're an amazing person, Aurora. Everyone here at Thirsty's would do anything for you. You've earned that respect by the way you run the place and the way you treat people."

She smiled at that and dipped her chin. "Thank you, Ryan, that means a lot."

He reached across and took her hand, thumb caressing her butter-soft skin before he pressed his lips to her knuckles and spoke again.

"But that's not what I admire most about you." He turned her palm up and raised her wrist to his face, inhaling her scent, subtle traces of jasmine perfume interwoven with the heady scent of a sexy, vibrant woman making his nostrils flare and moisture pool in his mouth. He pressed his mouth against the delicate skin of her wrist and tasted her slowly, circling his tongue, watching her eyes darken and hearing her breath catch. Heat pooled in his groin and the muscles in his chest tightened. Going slow was going to be torture, but so rewarding. He released her hand. When he spoke, his voice sounded rough, raw.

"You're passionate. I like that. I like that a lot." He held her gaze. "Finish your burger. Then there's another place I want to take you."

* * *

*A*urora locked the door to Thirsty's with shaky fingers. The neon pink sign winked farewell into the dark night and cast a glow over Ryan's face that drew attention to the strength of his features. She'd lusted after the teenager, but the man in front of her was another prospect entirely. Not only was he well built in places that made her inner vixen sit up and pay attention, she found his quiet confidence and raw masculinity compelling. Changes in her had sharpened her desire to a new edge too. She was already burning up. Did she have enough condoms? Hard on the heels of that thought, she stopped, remembering the state of her place as she'd rushed out that morning.

Ryan grabbed her hand and pulled her forward. "We're not going to your place tonight." He laughed softly. "I can see you thinking. Stop. Just trust me." He slid his leg over the seat of his motorbike and handed her the spare helmet. "Get on."

Aurora's heart squeezed at the directness of his approach. He was a man on a mission. And she did trust him. Her last niggle of doubt evaporated. He wanted this as much as she did. Her decision had been made on the mountain. However this ended, she promised herself, she'd have no regrets. Sliding the helmet on, she settled behind Ryan and pressed her breasts and torso against his back for the sheer pleasure of his low growl of approval, wrapping her arms around him and flattening her palms against the muscled ridges of his stomach.

Ryan's arms momentarily pressed over hers, hugging them against him, then the engine quietly rumbled to life and they rode off slowly down the main street. There was no traffic, and the darkness felt like a cloak of intimacy, wrapping them together like they were the only two people in the world.

Ryan rode to the edge of town and out one of the newer

roads, where the terrain was gently hilly, with small acreage lots. He rode over a cattle grid and down a gravel road, past an agricultural shed and behind a stand of gum trees, pulling up outside a timber cottage, shadowy in the night, with light dimly glowing through windows.

Aurora could just make out a few steps that lead up to a timber deck. The scent of freshly-sawn timber reached her as she lifted her visor and removed her helmet while Ryan killed the engine. She waited for him to hop off and shook out her hair, anticipation sending her nerves thrumming.

Ryan waited for her to slide off and kicked down the stand, parking the motorbike. He took the helmet from her hands, jogged up the steps and placed both helmets by the door, triggering an outside sensor light. He crouched to lift the doormat and produced a key, then slid it into the lock, the click loud in the silence.

A flutter of anticipation teased her nerves as Ryan turned off the exterior light and the door swung open, the soft light showing off a gorgeous room that would have thrilled her if she had eyes for anything but Ryan.

"Coming?" His voice was gruff, and it felt like his fingers were already running up and down her bare skin. She shivered in reaction.

"I'm hoping to. Give me a minute." She giggled and met him at the door.

He didn't laugh, just pulled her to him and held her close. He wrapped his arms around her and tucked her head under his chin, holding until she relaxed against him, giving a small sigh. His hands caressed her back then framed her face. "I'm desperate to be with you, but there's no pressure. Hell, you might change your mind in five minutes' time, and I'm okay with that. I'm just grateful you're here now. It's enough."

She swallowed against a lump of emotion in her throat.

She leaned back, her eyes searching his face, finding only honesty and desire there.

"You're a good man. I promise to stop making jokes, if you promise to take me to bed." Placing her hands on his chest, Aurora could feel his heart beating fast under her palms, mirroring the drumbeat of her own. She rose on her toes, the soft smile on her lips meeting the answering one on his as his head lowered.

The rasp of his day-old whiskers scraped at her skin, sending frissons of sensation spiraling. Her tongue sought entry to the warmth of his mouth, and the taste of him and the contact with his tongue sent a jolt of lightning straight to her feminine core.

Ryan's arms tightened around her as he deepened the kiss, his mouth claiming her and returning her exploration, angling his head, tasting and teasing as though it might be the last kiss of his life and he needed to imprint it deep in his memory.

Without breaking contact, he turned his body to move them through the door and close it behind them. She barely registered the move, her senses focused on exploration—the texture of his hair as her fingers gently raked his scalp, the tang of salt on the warm skin at his neck as she tasted his flesh. Reaching between them she yanked his t-shirt from his jeans and heard the hiss of his intake of breath as her hands moved over his abdomen, fingers brushing the shape of his muscles and the trail of hair from his belly button.

Ryan broke their kiss and hauled his shirt over his head, dropping it to the floor. "Let me help," he muttered, his fingers tugging at her polo shirt.

Aurora raised her arms so he could slip it from her body.

His groan of appreciation thrilled her. "You're killing me here."

He traced a finger along the red lace where the bra met

her flesh. "So, expect retaliation." Then his fingers found the hard peak of her nipples pressing against the lace and he traced circles of torment that sent her trembling.

She gasped as he pinched each nipple then bent his head to suck and lick each taut bud through the fabric in turn. Pleasure radiated through her body as he finally palmed each breast, thumbs caressing her aching nipples. She bit her lip and he raised his head to kiss her again, his mouth warm and wet and so full of teasing intent.

As they kissed, her hands roamed his chest and she felt his pec muscles twitch as she ran her fingers over his nipples, then scraped her nails gently across them. At his sharp intake of breath, a haze of sensual appreciation washed over her.

Still kissing, his hands snaked behind her and released her bra, his fingers dragging down the straps until it was free, and he dropped it to the floor. When her breasts were naked at last, his hands repeated their trail of discovery until she whimpered.

They broke the kiss, both breathing fast, and Ryan leaned his forehead against hers.

"I wanted to make this slow. I don't know if that's going to be possible," he whispered.

"Slow is overrated. We can try that next time."

Ryan huffed out a laugh and raised his head, his eyes glittery in the dim light. "Done."

She reached for his belt buckle at the same time he reached for her jeans snap. They raced to undress each other, chuckling as they fumbled, then abandoning those efforts to race at shucking off their own clothes.

As Aurora shimmied out of her red lace panties, she heard Ryan groan, but her eyes were riveted to the sight of his erection as his trunks hit the floor. His cock was ready, a bead of moisture at the tip of his circumcised penis standing proud of his trimmed pubic hair, his balls ready for her palm. Her intake of breath was involuntary. Her mouth suddenly dry, she licked her lips and forced her gaze to his face.

His expression was calm, but a pulse beat at his neck.

She stood and gave his body a leisurely scan, the flush rising across her skin giving away the truth. She wanted this with an intensity that was not casual. Those were the words they'd told each other; but here, naked and raw and ready, slick with her own desire, there was every chance walking away from each other might be harder than either of them was prepared to admit.

No regrets. She held his gaze and reached out.

He stilled and let her take his shaft in her hand, their eyes locked.

His jaw tightened, but he let her take control, and she smiled with wicked intent.

She stroked up and down slowly, took the weight of his balls in her other hand, cupping them and releasing them. Finally, she thumbed the bead of moisture at the tip, smearing it and circling the sensitive slit, then raised her thumb to her mouth and licked it before taking her thumb in her mouth to suck.

* * *

*D*ying. He was definitely … dying. The groan he heard was his, but he didn't recognize the sound, it was ripped from so deep in his chest as Aurora's big green eyes, pupils black with desire, stared him down as she slid her thumb, slick with his juice, into her mouth.

Emotion ripped through his chest, like she'd reached in there and grabbed his heart, not his cock. *It wasn't supposed to be like this.* It was supposed to be fun and flirty and sexy and light-hearted and satisfying as hell because they'd already established chemistry was not their problem. Timing was, history was, never attraction. But emotion? He was blind-sided by feelings interwoven with the burning ache to possess her.

He wanted Aurora quaking with need and as desperate as him, but he hoped like hell she wasn't feeling what he was feeling, this feeling of *rightness* and *connection* as well as the firestorm of need. Because she had no future with him, and she deserved someone who had the capacity to love her.

He couldn't do that, but he could give her an orgasm that would blow her mind. The scent of her arousal filled his nostrils and he pulled Aurora into his arms, claiming her mouth in a fierce kiss. He walked her backwards to the kitchen counter, mouths still tasting and hungry, grabbing her naked butt and lifting her up onto the benchtop. She gasped a little against his mouth and squirmed, nipping at his bottom lip in retaliation as he slowed the pace, then pulled away from his lips, breathing hard as he trailed his fingers over the softness of her abdomen and caressed the curve of her hips.

"Ryan!" she whimpered, her fingers digging into his shoulders. "I want more."

God, how she turned him on! He looked up at her, her face tight with need, and dropped to his knees between her legs then lifted her thighs over his shoulders.

"Oh yes, I want that ..." she panted.

She opened fully to him, bracing herself against the wall behind her with her shoulders, and her hands clenching on the curved edge of the laminate bench top. He slid a thumb down from her mound and parted her folds, slick with her arousal, using the moisture to circle her throbbing clit. Her hissed intake of breath was his reward and his cock twitched, hard.

"You're so beautiful ..." His words a prayer of gratitude.

He slid a finger into her moist core and watched her face tighten with need.

"Oh God, oh God … oh my God …"

Her moans urged him on, but he wanted to draw this out so she never forgot this night. He teased her with the slow, firm, slide of his fingers, in and out.

She bit her lip, her eyes closed, lost in a fog of sensual concentration.

He stepped up the pace and used his other thumb to work her clit at the same time so he could watch her face. He could feel her tension coiling and her legs begin to shake as her world contracted to that small tight nub.

Finally, when his heart and his cock were ready to explode, he placed his mouth where his fingers had been, circling her throbbing clit and tasting her juices, plunging his tongue deep into her core, responding to her cues until he knew her orgasm was his to claim.

Her fingers clenched in his hair, pressing him against her, and there was no place else in the world he wanted to be when she plunged over the edge and jerked and pulsed against his mouth with his name on her lips.

* * *

Stars exploded behind her eyelids and her whole body convulsed as Ryan gripped her hips and laved his tongue around her clit and vagina. Somehow, she didn't slide off the counter. The orgasm that ripped through her was the most powerful of her life. Tears from some burst of emotion she couldn't contain or understand leaked from the corner of her eyes. Aurora could do nothing about it. She was spent, and yet desperate to feel Ryan's cock and her warmth pulsing around him. She curled her fingers in his hair and forced his head up as her vagina clenched in another wave.

"I need you inside me, now!"

His eyes flashed fire and he wiped his hand across his mouth as he leaped to his feet. He fished in his jeans for a condom and handed it to her.

She ripped it open with trembling fingers.

He tore it from her hands and sheathed himself, then grabbed her face in his hands, thumbing away the tears before kissing her with intense and tender possession. Then he gathered her close and she tilted her hips and wrapped her legs around him.

The moment she took him inside, another orgasm began to build, and she gasped and braced her shoulders against the wall behind her, rocking her hips as he began to thrust and retreat into her tight eager flesh.

"Look at me."

Her eyes flew open and their gazes locked. It was the hottest moment of her life. Aurora had a healthy enjoyment of sex, but nothing had prepared her for how raw and exposed she felt as Ryan's eyes bored into hers and his jaw clenched, the cords in his neck standing out.

He wanted her to see he wasn't hiding. Emotion, intense and honest, played across his features, mirroring her own turmoil. Understanding crashed through her. He was showing her this wasn't a game, this was real.

He wanted this too. All of it, the heat and the lust and the messy emotion too.

She locked her ankles around him.

"Come and … get me …" She arched and thrust hard against him.

At her challenge, the heat in his eyes blazed and he gave her what she wanted, what she needed, hard and fast, his sweat-sheened face intent and determined, until she was almost sobbing with need.

Then, at last, Ryan reached his hand between them to stroke her swollen pulsing nub and she whimpered and shattered completely, her fingers digging into his biceps.

Moments later he let out a cry as he came hard, his chest and shoulders heaving, rocking slowly in and out a few more times before he gathered her to him, their hearts racing and breathing jagged and panting. He kissed her then, the taste of her own arousal on his lips, a deep lingering kiss of tender connection.

Even as she sank into the feeling, an inner voice warned to guard her heart, because where Ryan was concerned, what she felt and what was true should not be trusted.

CHAPTER 9

*A*urora woke to the sensation of a large warm hand cupping her breast, slowly thumbing her nipple, and sending shafts of awareness spearing to the juncture of her thighs.

Ryan.

A smile on her lips, she stretched luxuriantly and rolled toward the man tracing lazy circles around the tight nub of flesh, reveling in the tension coiling in the pit of her belly and the half smile on his rugged face. She reached up to slide her palm against the roughness of his beard, the rasp sending shivers of reaction across her skin.

Dawn lent a pearly glow to the room, and her heart sighed as he lowered his lips to hers and his hand slid to her hip, tracing a line down her leg, then between her thighs, passion reigniting like lightning on tinder-dry brush.

Later, she awoke from a deep sleep to discover she was tucked into his side like she'd been made for him, one leg draped over his thighs while he slept, dark lashes against his cheeks, mouth slightly parted. Her leg was pale against his tanned skin. As she felt the slow rise and fall of his chest, the tight band that habitually held her chest prisoner loosened a notch. As worried as she was for her brother, her mother, Thirsty's, and the music festival, with Ryan by her side, the burden seemed somehow less daunting. She closed her eyes for a moment to daydream.

"I gotta take a picture of that."

Her eyes blinked open.

Ryan was smiling at her, finger tracing a small strawberry mark on her abdomen, above her trimmed pubic hair. Something about him was different this morning. That edge he carried was absent. Her influence? It gave her a warm glow. He reached past her to the bedside table for his phone and she chuckled and batted away his hand, sliding on top of him.

"Or, I could take a dick pic of you to add to my collection," she teased, pressing her breasts into Ryan's chest as she made a grab for her phone, squealing in mock outrage as he pinched her butt, making her fumble.

The phone slipped from her grasp and slid along the mattress, but Ryan ignored it, a low growl rumbling through his chest.

"Not happening, you wench." He wrapped his arms around her and rolled, flipping her, laughing, onto her back, the sheets sliding down to his hips as he rose on his arms above her.

"Whatcha gunna do about it, big guy?" Aurora reached her hands up to grab Ryan's face, about to pull his lips to hers for another smoldering kiss when she froze.

Davey's voice cut the air.

"Sis, is that you?" Her brother's face appeared on the screen, his eyes wide with uncertainty.

Ryan's face fell so fast it would have been comical, except it wasn't. It was awful. He glanced over her shoulder and swore, the lit phone screen bright in the low light.

"Ryan, why are … What's going on?" Davey's voice sounded part angry, part confused.

Ryan rolled away and Aurora grabbed the phone, lifting the sheet over herself.

She'd bump-dialed her brother, the last number on her phone because she'd been redialing habitually just to hear his recorded voice message, sometimes using an app, whatever she hadn't tried last. But he was live. His face filled the screen. A surge of relief overwhelmed her.

"Davey, you've got your phone back. Oh my God, it's so good to see you. I've been so worried." Tears pricked her eyes. He was alive. She sucked in a gulp. Her subconscious had doubted it.

It was full daylight where he was, some kind of farm, but the coastline was blue behind him in the distance. Green rolling hills. Pretty, but she only had eyes for her brother. His beard was gone and his wild-man hair too, and his face looked softer. She hadn't realized how much he'd changed until she saw him looking more like the Davey of old. But he was looking past her, a frown on his brow.

"Ryan? Is that you? Seriously? You and Aurora? What's going on? Did you tell her?"

Behind her Ryan slid off the bed and began gathering strewn clothes and a chill settled over her. *Tell her what?*

* * *

*R*yan stepped into his jeans and pulled his t-shirt over his head, frustration making his movements jerky. This was bad. He'd hoped for more time to explore this … whatever it was … with Aurora to see if she felt any of the things that had crept up on him during the night. It hadn't just been lust, for either of them. But that hope died the moment Davey had uttered his query. Whatever Ryan said now was going to sound like a lie. He turned, and as expected, Aurora's face telegraphed her emotions. She was bracing for more bad news, even in her relief at the chance to talk to her brother.

Guilt twisted the knife in his belly. Aurora didn't need him, she needed her brother, whole and well and returned to her. Wanting more was a mistake; he should have learned that from his father. He had no place here. He was the outsider.

"Tell me what? Davey, forget about me and Ryan, please, tell me what's happening with you? Are you okay? That's all that matters." Aurora held the phone away from her face so she could see her brother, the sheet tucked under her arms to cover her.

Ryan picked up her shirt and draped it over her naked shoulders. On the small screen, Davey saw him and looked away, shaking his head. When his gaze returned, his expression was weighted with regret.

"I'm so sorry I left you in the lurch, sis. I just had to go. I'm okay. Well, not yet, but I will be, eventually. I'm where I need to be."

He heard Aurora's sharp intake and saw her shoulders hunch tighter. He moved to sit on the edge of the bed, not touching her, but close enough to see and be seen.

Davey's gaze bounced between them.

"But I'm glad you're both there. Aurora, you need to know something. You too, Ryan. I've got to start making things right."

A sense of foreboding filled him. Davey wasn't ready to be making decisions. It was too soon. Beside him, he felt Aurora stiffen.

"Jesus, Davey, you're not in trouble with the law, are you?"

Davey shook his head.

"No. But that's thanks to Ryan. He … bailed me out before

that could happen. I'm sorry, Aurora. It was me taking the missing cash. And I spent the loan you gave me too, and the business line of credit. It's all gone. I told myself they were just short-term personal loans that I'd pay back to the business, but it just grew and grew until there was nothing left. That was the shock that made me reach rock bottom. Aurora, the money that's in the line of credit now keeping the business afloat is all Ryan's. As far as I'm concerned, he owns Thirsty's Bar and Grill."

Aurora's hand flew to her mouth, and she turned her face to him with anger, dismay, and hurt in every line of her expression.

Ryan held up his hands to stop his old friend. "Davey, you don't need to do this. That's a loan, we can sort it out when you're well. It's still your pub. Now is not the time for this decision," he insisted.

But Davey just shook his head.

"I can't go back there. I can't have this hanging over me while I get treatment. I don't want it, and Aurora, you deserve the truth. And Mum. I'll tell her when she gets back. I hope you can forgive me one day. When the festival is over, I'm selling the pub. It's the only way out. I'll pay you back eventually, I promise. I'm so sorry."

Aurora twisted and turned her back to him. When she spoke, the hurt and grief for her brother in her voice pummeled him.

"Oh, Davey. This is ... I can't believe you didn't talk to me. There might have been other solutions."

Solutions that didn't involve him.

She glanced across at Ryan like he was a stranger she was seeing for the first time.

It was a punch to the gut. And he'd done it to himself when he kept his deal with Davey a secret. Aurora had a right to know about the money he'd loaned and his stake as a silent partner. She'd done nothing but stand by her brother and been honest with Ryan about her attraction.

He'd persuaded himself that they'd made no commitment, but he now knew how badly he'd stuffed up and hurt people he cared about. He'd let down Davey and the whole Conroy family, Aurora most of all. Realization hit him like an Outback road train. He wanted more with Aurora than sex. He wanted that connection he'd felt last night to be part of his life. And he might have had a chance if he'd been straight with her from the start. She might have made different choices about him, he realized now. It wasn't his call. He'd taken that opportunity from her. Lines were not blurred between them; they were crystal clear.

She couldn't even look at him. Her priority was not him, or the business, it was her brother. She lifted and lowered a shoulder, her voice soft as she spoke to her brother with love.

"It's done now. You did what you needed to do. Don't worry about the business, or me. It's only money. Just worry about yourself. Focus on getting well and let the future take care of itself, okay? I've got it under control. Right, Ryan?" She looked at him now, steel in her gaze.

He took her hint. When he spoke, there was no indication of his turmoil, only quiet confidence. He could at least allay Davey's fears.

"Aurora's got the place running like a dream. She doesn't need me. She's right, focus on your health. Nothing else matters."

Davey glanced between them. "I know you can run the place, Aurora. But the bank can pull the line of credit at any time if they have concerns about their investment. Just promise me you'll keep your money there, Ryan, until I can get the place sold."

Ryan felt like he'd been punched. He'd made it clear to

Davey from the start that the loan was no strings attached. Was Davey upset because he'd seen him with Aurora?

"I don't need the money." His voice was stiff. "There's no way I'd pull it. I've seen your sister at work."

Aurora turned to him, her nostrils flared and her jaw tight.

The knife in his gut twisted. It was clear that she hated his money being in their family business. And now he wished it weren't. There was no going back to the way things were. "It can stay there forever as far as I'm concerned. Just get well, Davey, that's all I want." Then he moved away and began locking up the cottage.

Aurora ended the call by blowing her brother a kiss. As the screen went black a kookaburra outside heralded the day, his wild laughter a savage commentary on good intentions gone horribly wrong.

As the cry faded to silence it sparked Aurora into action. She leaped to her feet and spun to face him, angrily struggling into her t-shirt, and then grabbing a bed cushion to throw at his head. He caught it instead, which only incited her rage.

"I cannot believe you, Ryan Harrington. How bloody dare you treat me like an idiot and not tell me you were invested in the business? Why did you lie about that?" She stalked around the room, the jiggle of her naked butt stirring his blood even as she eyed him with cold fury. She scrambled past him, rummaging on the floor for her underwear like the place was on fire and she needed to escape.

He gathered the scraps of red lace she hadn't seen him place on the end of the bed.

When she turned and saw them dangling from her fingers, she snatched them like they were toxic.

"Will you calm down for a second, Red?"

"Calm down? Calm down? Why the heck would I do that?

And do NOT call me that. You do not get to call me that. You can take me home right now and then get on your bike and go back where you came from."

"Will you just let me explain?"

"There's nothing to explain. You lied to me, you're rich enough to buy a pub at the drop of a hat, and you get your kicks hanging around to play temporary barman while you let me run it for you. You must have been laughing your guts out. You get to play the hero solving my staffing problems for me, when all you really had to do was snap your fingers. Must be nice to be you." Scorn dripped from her words. "Oh, and the icing on the cake? All this." She gestured wildly around the room. "You let me think *I* was convincing *you*. It really couldn't be more perfect for you, could it? A shame you got caught out."

He folded his arms across his chest as she struggled into her jeans, shoving her underwear into the pockets.

"If you'd just listen for a minute ..."

"That's a hard 'no' from me. If I could order an Uber out here, I'd make my own way home, but I can't, and I have too much work to do putting on a festival in a couple of days that this town is depending on. So, if you'll just shut-up ... I'd like to go now." She walked to the door and stood there, arms crossed, glaring at him.

He walked to her. Her hair was wild, her eyes blazed, and her chest, unencumbered by her bra, rose and fell under the t-shirt. Even wishing him dead, she turned him on.

She was lashing out, hurting him like she'd been hurt. But he couldn't let her go unchallenged, for all the good it would do him. There was no coming back from this.

"That's not how it was. It was never about the money. I'm sorry that I didn't tell you about the loan. That was a mistake. I thought you had enough on your plate. I should have realized it wasn't my call to make. My bad. And this"—he flicked his hand to encompass the room—"was two consenting adults. This was a man and a woman having a damn good time giving each other pleasure, remember? I'm sorry that's not enough for you. I guess that makes me an idiot too."

And he walked out the door.

CHAPTER 10

*E*xhaustion was catching up with her. The lack of sleep last night, the emotional roller-coaster talking to Davey, and the early start all crept up on Aurora as the afternoon heat peaked. She longed for a nap, but crews were arriving to set up the musicians' camp and she was needed outside to direct them.

Sighing heavily, she slid on her sunglasses over bloodshot eyes and jammed a Thirsty's-logoed cap on over her curls. She'd grab an energy drink and get the site set-up sorted first, then sneak away for a twenty-minute catnap. She prayed when she did, there would be no dreaming of the pleasure she'd found in Ryan's arms. That would be too cruel. Of all the shocks of the day, the discovery that he'd been lying to her was the worst.

When Davey dumped his bombshell, Ryan's expression of guilt had shredded her. If Davey hadn't needed to hear words of support from her, she would have torn strips off them both. Davey for thinking she needed protecting from the truth, the habit of a lifetime that needed to stop. But Ryan's collusion, she been blind-sided by. She'd chewed the inside of her cheek raw biting back what she wanted to say, but there really was no choice but to suck it up while Davey's health was her priority. She had a lawyer looking into it, and only the thought that she was going to pay back every cent Ryan had loaned Davey as fast as she could was keeping her on her feet now, stepping out into the blazing sun.

"Hey, Red, gotta minute?"

Aurora turned to face Ryan. He was stacking kegs by the storeroom, patches of sweat staining his shirt. She hadn't seen him since that morning. A traitorous part of her, the wanton lonely part that hadn't been out to play in an awfully long time, wanted to rush over and grab on tight, take comfort in his solid grounding presence. The furious hurt-woman-who'd-been-lied-to part simply wanted to kill him. Lucky for Ryan, the newly crowned solo-businesswoman-with-a-mountain-of-debt part was in charge. She wasn't giving him the satisfaction of seeing her lose her cool again.

"I thought we'd discussed that?" This time her voice was cool. "It's Aurora. Especially now we're … business associates." At least until she could arrange new finance. She already had a broker friend in Sydney making enquiries. The company accounts would look a lot healthier after the festival, she crossed her fingers.

Ryan straightened from his task and put his hands on his hips. A part of his anatomy she'd had her legs wrapped around with gusto in the night.

She stiffened her spine. "Listen, I know we need to talk, but not now. I've got to get the site organized for the trucks coming in. It's been a long day already." She gestured with her hand, waving between them. "This"—she paused, sucked in a steadying breath to quell the tremble she hated hearing in her voice—"this is just going to have to wait."

Ryan nodded and ran his hand along his jaw. He hadn't shaved. He looked tired too, and wary. She'd seen that look before, back when he was a teenager, like he was bracing for something bad.

"Fine. Aurora. Can I just say one thing?"

She nodded stiffly, not wanting to go, not wanting to stay, biting her lip to stop tears from sneaking out. God, she hated being an emotional mess. Hated him for turning her into one.

"Well, its two things. One is I'm sorry for not telling you straight up. I was wrong and I see that now. And two, you get to call all the shots from here. That's it."

Anger flared, hot and hard. She strode over and jabbed a finger into Ryan's chest. He didn't flinch.

"Well, how bloody generous of you. Listen, you don't get to give me permission for anything, or escape that lightly. It's too bloody late for a crisis of conscience. We'll talk when I'm good and ready, and we'll talk as equals. You don't get to pin sorting out this mess on me. Got it?"

Something glinted in his eye and the corners of his mouth flickered, but he nodded.

"Got it … Aurora."

As she turned away, she cursed herself for giving up too soon on researching his past and vowed to remedy that when she got a minute, but for now she had other priorities.

* * *

The midnight sky was bleak and desolate, scattering clouds obscuring the moon and stars. An hour riding over unfenced Outback highways kept Ryan focused on the bitumen, scanning for wandering livestock or wildlife intent on jumping into his path, likely fatal for both. He felt the absence of Aurora nestled against his back, her arms tight around his waist, like a physical ache. Finally, he turned down a narrow gravel road, well-tended with only a small sign to point the way to the tiny airfield, lit by temporary beacons. The company jet was being refueled as he arrived. He left the bike in a small hanger and climbed aboard. Inside, a laptop loaded with reports from Tracey awaited for him to sift through.

It made for grim reading. By the time he touched down in Melbourne two hours later, he had a plan to execute. He fired off a brief distracted text to Aurora asking her to call, grateful the handover crew were arriving that morning, and headed to his penthouse for a few hours' sleep. The immaculately kept apartment offered sparkling panoramic views of the city's night skyline. But it offered none of the serenity he'd experienced in brief moments under that vast Outback sky over the past two weeks. He turned on the shower, filling the bathroom with steam. In the mirror, a stranger with bleak ice-blue eyes stared back until steam mercifully obscured his face.

Hours later dawn broke and he rose, showered, and shaved. He donned the first suit his hand touched from the row waiting in his dressing room and grabbed a selection of ties. The stiff shirt was bespoke and cost a bomb, but the collar felt tight around his neck and he contemplated ditching the tie. He checked his phone. No call yet from Aurora.

At seven, the penthouse elevator pinged and Tracey walked briskly in, her beige pumps clicking on the porcelain tiles, all understated elegance from her neat cream suit to her immaculate gray-streaked blunt bob, calm smile in place but new lines of tension around her eyes.

"The pale blue, not the orange. Matches your eyes. Just put it on and forget about it. Here's your coffee. David sends his regards."

He finished knotting the blue tie and accepted the coffee.

He took a sip; long black and the perfect temperature, just as he liked it.

"Thank you, Tracey. And thank David. Sorry to ruin your planned trip."

She tsked. "You'll make it up to us, you always do." She scanned him up and down. "Something's different." Her gaze narrowed. "Did you meet someone?"

He stiffened. "How the hell did you get that idea?"

She pursed her lips then smiled. "Instincts of a blood-hound, remember?"

"Hmmm. Shame I didn't have you do the due diligence on the casino acquisition."

"I think forensic accounting skills might have been required for that one," she said, her tone dry. "Does she know what she's getting into?"

He didn't answer. There was nothing to say. If Aurora saw a future with him, she hadn't given him any signals. The opposite in fact. She'd been up for the sex, but only in the context of their dare. He couldn't blame her. And now he'd been forced to leave her in the lurch the day before the music festival without a handover. It didn't matter how good Jack and his crew were, she'd feel betrayed. And after the hurry he'd left in ten years ago, there was a strong chance she might never forgive him. But he couldn't afford to think about that now. The welfare of thousands of employees was at stake; his personal happiness would have to wait.

"Can we just focus on today please?"

Soon he'd surrender his gray man persona and come out of the shadows into the bright hot glare of a press conference. Thanks to Aurora, he was at peace with that. She'd shown him how to graciously accept responsibility for circumstances outside your control, and face challenges head on, without flinching.

His executive assistant smiled and nodded, a pleased look on her face. "Certainly."

* * *

The next morning Aurora woke in a daze, horrified to discover she must have slept through her early alarm. Yesterday's bump-in had been exhausting and run late into the night. She'd only seen Ryan at a distance twice in the afternoon, for which she'd been grateful, her wounds too raw to hide. She grabbed her phone to discover it was completely flat—she'd somehow turned off the charger at the wall when she fell into bed. Setting it to charge, she took a quick shower to wake up, slicked on mascara and lip gloss and scrunched some product into her damp curls, then donned her Muster in the Dust volunteer team t-shirt in lurid green with matching event coordinator lanyard. Filling her KeepCup with espresso, she hurried over to Thirsty's to check Ryan had matters in hand there before she headed to the event team's temporary office at the council chambers. Her phone showed a missed call, but she didn't stop to return it. She could see Ryan on the way.

Gwen tried to hail her, but Aurora didn't stop and entered the office without knocking, only to stop sharply. A stranger was seated at the desk, talking on the phone. He glanced at her and held up a finger. Irritation and confusion melded with fear. What the hell was going on?

"She's here now, do you want me to put her on? Okay, I'll email you later. Sorry, I'm Jack." He handed her his phone with an apologetic look. "It's Ryan. I'll be back in a minute." He left swiftly, and Aurora's nerves tensed.

"Ryan, what's up?" Nothing good, she already knew.

"Aurora, glad I reached you ..."

"What do you mean? Reach me? I'm not hard to find."

"Look there's no easy way to say this, and I can't talk long as I'm about to go into a meeting, but something urgent came up last night. I'm in Melbourne. Jack's my best site-manager, he'll step into my shoes."

Her stomach crashed to the floor.

"You're kidding me, right?"

His departure was what she'd craved short weeks ago, but it had been impossible to foresee how much the reality would feel like a betrayal. Acid rose in her throat as Ryan continued speaking.

"Jack will run Thirsty's during the festival; you can count on him and his team. I'm sorry, Aurora. It's not what I planned, but it was outside my control. We can talk after the festival and after I've managed my work problem. I'll call later when I can."

There was a beat of silence and the last pieces of Aurora's heart broke. He'd left. She was on her own.

"That won't be necessary. Goodbye, Ryan."

She ended the call.

CHAPTER 11

*M*ain Street in Granite Ridge was pumping, music alternating from stages at either end. Aurora saw smiling faces everywhere. The Muster in the Dust music festival was a huge hit, and the only thing that could have trumped it as a triumph was breaking of the drought. As luck would have it, rain arrived in the form of a small thunderstorm overnight that washed off the top layer of dust. It didn't break the drought, but it put smiles on tired faces as the last day kicked off. Even the kookaburras were laughing with joy.

Aurora smiled along with everyone else, but it was an act of determination. Everyone had worked so hard to put on this event, she wasn't going to hint at her inner misery. Ryan had gone, and taken her foolish heart with him.

"Hey, Aurora, glad I caught you before I go on stage." Jazzy Parker, her childhood friend and now Mayor Jasmine Parker, appeared through the crowd and squeezed her in a quick hug. "This is the best thing to happen to Granite Ridge since the B&S ball was invented. And it's all down to you, no one else could have pulled this off. You don't want a job at the council, do you? We could do with an events team. If you stick around, I'm going to get you to run my next Mayoral campaign."

Aurora laughed and blinked away the tears that sprang to her eyes. "You don't need my help, hon. You'll romp it in."

"Aw, babe, don't you cry, or I'll lose it too." Jazzy sniffed and laughed and glanced around. "Where's Ryan? I want to thank him too. He's been amazing. You two make a great team."

Aurora plastered on a happy face, determined not to kill the Mayor's vibe. She worked so hard for her community. She deserved to enjoy the event's success and bask in the moment. "He had to go at short notice, some work emergency."

Jazzy didn't say anything but gave her another hug and whispered in her ear. "I'm sure he'll be back."

Aurora just bit her lip and shooed her old friend away. "Never mind me, they're waiting for you on stage to intro the final act and close this shindig. Knock 'em dead."

Her friend grinned and hurried off.

Aurora cheered louder than anyone else as Jazzy walked onto the main stage and waved to the five thousand strong crowd. The festival was a financial success on ticket sales alone before the first night was over, but the real success was giving the townsfolk a reason to believe they could pull off the event and give visitors something to talk about when they went home. Hope was the most precious commodity on offer, and two years into the drought, it was priceless.

Her careful spreadsheet plan had delivered the right resources to the right places when needed in mostly the right quantities. They used all the contingency supplies, but that was fine—that's what contingencies were for. Enough food, drink, and temporary accommodation had arrived to keep bellies full and spirits high. The tent and caravan city in the showgrounds flowed along neat rows as pegged out by the show committee volunteers. Massive hired generators supplied the extra power needed, and water stations and temporary amenities blocks everywhere kept people hydrated and comfortable in the heat. A fleet of courtesy buses ran people in a loop between the campground, food trucks, music tents, and stages. All the music talent turned up when and where they needed to be, including an impromptu jam session on the main stage with the headline act, a former resident who'd gone on to conquer the national and international country rock scene, a didgeridoo player, and a bagpipe band. The crowd had gone nuts. And through it all the locals worked volunteer-run stalls and put out the welcome mat with pride.

Aurora could not have been prouder of what had been achieved and her small part in it. But it couldn't fill the hollowness inside that her brother had missed it all, and so had Ryan. One she couldn't call, and one she couldn't speak to—it hurt too much, letting his calls go to messages. She couldn't afford to fall apart until this was over in a few hours.

As the final fireworks ignited, she turned to leave and spied police sergeant Jim Adams, so she tapped him on the shoulder.

"Thanks for letting me know about the drug bust, Jim. The security team appreciated the heads up. Any other problems I need to know about?"

The officer shook his head. "Nah. We got lucky with the timing of the tip off about Gareth's place. We had time to organize the raids, seize a lot of drugs, and put some drug traffickers before the courts. I'm not kidding myself; we chop off one head, another tends to spring up in its place. Just not in time to affect this event, thankfully. We've had a few drunk and disorderly, some party drugs seized, a rise in break and enters, but nothing we couldn't handle. Happy days," he ended with a wry smile.

"I'm glad," said Aurora, relieved Davey was far away.

A wave of exhaustion washed over her as the final act kicked off. Suddenly Aurora couldn't bear to be among the celebrations a moment longer. She pushed her way through the crowd to the side entry at Thirsty's and made her way to the office, grateful that she'd seen Jack, Ryan's right hand man, who'd proved as capable as promised, out enjoying the festivities so she had it to herself. Closing the door behind her, she slumped on the couch Davey kept there. She hadn't seen the news in days, so she flicked open her phone to see what kind of coverage the festival was getting.

Thumbing through the newsfeed a headline pulled her wide awake. *Reclusive CEO steals from workers.* Expecting to see a photo of a mining tycoon, she was winded to see a picture of a face she knew intimately instead. *Ryan Harrington, publicity shy owner of HLR Group,* read the caption. She read the article with mounting horror. This was Ryan's work emergency? He *owned* HLR? Australia's biggest hospitality, leisure, and resort business? One of his businesses has been underpaying workers for two years? Nothing about the story made any sense, so she clicked on a video news link.

Ryan, devastatingly handsome in a suit and tie, walking to a podium in a crowded press conference, lights blazing and cameras flashing, dark and dangerous and staring down the hungry media.

Aurora's heart lurched even as her body responded with heat to the way his broad shoulders filled out the custom suit. It was a feeding frenzy. How could he stand it?

Ryan stood, calm and composed, and simply waited for the clamor of questions to peter out into silence, scanning the room. When the room finally quietened, he spoke, his voice firm and authoritative, as though the rabble had not happened.

Aurora was on the edge of her seat.

"Thank you for your time today, ladies and gentlemen. My name is Ryan Harrington. I am owner of HLR Group. I'll be making a short statement and then I'll take some questions." His deep voice sent ripples of reaction down her spine. He focused on the camera now, talking to the audience at home as much as the media pack.

"Firstly, my priority today is to reassure the staff of HLR Group's recent acquisition, this casino, and all our other enterprises, that respecting workers' entitlements is non-negotiable. All workers will receive everything they are owed." He paused to emphasize the point.

"HLR Group has set up a hotline for workers to get advice on their individual situations. That hotline is a permanent new addition to our existing channels. There will be no reason for any worker, past or present, to fear their claims will not be heard and taken seriously.

"The situation of underpayment of workers was made known to me two days ago. I'm not here to defend the indefensible. All workers entitlements will be paid in full within the next month. I've personally guaranteed the funds. We have assembled a special team to expedite payments.

"I've also established an audit team to investigate and ensure the high standards of HLR Group are being met across every arm of our business. That team will be independent and will report directly to me."

He outlined how the process would work, and then opened the floor to questions, calmly taking pointed questions that painted him as evil. *How did this scandal happen on your watch? What do you intend to do about it? Do you feel personally responsible for stealing workers' wages? HLR Group has thrived to become the most successful hospitality business in*

Australia by exploiting its workers. Does this affect plans to publicly list the company? How are you a fit and proper person to hold licenses if your workers are not being properly paid?

One female reporter from a current affairs program, who seemed to have a personal grudge, tried to hound him, but he treated her with the same courtesy as financial journalists.

"Chantelle Jones, News 24 Network. Mr. Harrington, you're one of the richest businessmen in Australia. How do you sleep at night?"

"I've lost a lot of sleep working on a solution since this issue was discovered. That's why we have this result today. Looking after workers in my priority."

She pressed him, her tone aggressive. "Why is it you haven't done personal interviews before this? What else do you have to hide?"

"Chantelle, I'm here to talk about the business. If you have any business questions, I'm happy to take them." He turned his head to another journalist. "I'll take another question. Yes, Bradley?"

The barrage continued.

Ryan in corporate tiger mode was a revelation. His answers were direct, his presence commanding. As the camera zoomed in on his eyes, Aurora saw behind the façade to the real hurt he felt. It wasn't for himself. It was his workers he cared about. The man who shunned publicity had taken the stage to make sure they knew he had their back. That was the Ryan she knew. The media had it all wrong.

Realization struck hard. He'd dealt with this his whole life, dealing with the judgement of others for actions he wasn't responsible for, starting with his father. No wonder he chose to guard his privacy closely. Yet in a crisis, he put his needs to one side to do what needed to be done.

It dawned on her that he didn't expect the same things

from life she had. While her family had shielded her to give her a happy sunny childhood, overprotective after the early loss of a father she didn't remember, he'd done well to simply survive his. The fact he'd made something of himself was a complete triumph. She'd learned she was worthy of love from being loved, but Ryan had yet to learn that lesson. He was busy trying to save Davey and her and everyone else he cared about, but who was trying to save him?

He'd lied to her—the lies of omission—but the need to protect himself now made sense. Their budding connection had blown up in their faces before he had a chance to trust it. Her refusal to listen to his explanations was another door slamming in his face. She might have ruined any chance for them, but he deserved to know the truth. He was worthy of love and she loved him. He needed to know that.

* * *

*R*yan stuffed his tie in his pocket and loosened his shirt neck. Two days of back to back meetings and briefings and he was done.

"I knew there was a reason I didn't do media. It sucks." The media furor hadn't abated. Journalists attempted doorstop interviews any time he left the building to go from one conference to another. Now they knew what the head of HLR Group looked like, his anonymity was shot.

Tracey shook her head. "You're a novelty. It won't last. Six weeks tops."

Ryan grunted. His face was out there now. It had never been a complete secret, but he'd preferred to let others take the limelight. Taking the stage was a small price to pay for doing the right thing, but it left him feeling like a caged animal. He longed for his motorbike and the chance to put some open road between him and the circus.

Tracey stood at the window and turned to face him, arms folded and expression serious. "We need to talk."

He frowned. Nothing good ever followed those four words coming from a woman, directed at him. Mostly someone seeking more than he could give. But he owed Tracey his attention, and so much more. She was looking at him fondly.

"Life is short. I'm ready to retire. I've hesitated because I worried about you. You seemed so cut off from people. I saw you becoming restless and I began to wonder. When you phoned a few weeks ago from the Outback, I could hear something new in your voice and I started to hope. When you came back to Melbourne, it was obvious.

"And the way you stepped out from the shadows these past few days has confirmed it. You've changed. I'm glad.

"You've always been good at big decisions, Ryan. Choosing to share your life with someone is the biggest one you will make. The right person by your side makes life sweet. I've got that with David. You deserve that. You've always deserved that, and I hope you choose that. And that's all I'm going to say. But speaking as a friend now, not your executive assistant, don't waste a chance at love. That's all I wanted to say. And we can talk about my finish date another day."

* * *

*A*fter Tracey left, Ryan sat for a long time at his office desk, with the lights off, staring out to the darkening night, watching as the sky faded to indigo and artificial lights lit up the office buildings around his.

He tried to imagine continuing with his life the way it used to be. And he knew with certainty he couldn't do it. The void inside would eventually swallow him up until he disappeared completely. No amount of long motorcycle rides in the night could fill that lonely well.

Then he thought of Aurora, in all her moods, from feisty to funny to flaming hot, and his lips began to curve. And the heart he'd never believed he had began to beat hard and fast and grow until it filled his chest.

He loved Aurora!

As the realization crashed through him, the moon slid out between two buildings, whole and huge and glowing with life.

Loving her had broken him out of his self-imposed solitude and dragged him into the light. The passion they'd shared burned so hot because it was founded on a deep connection. He knew her, and she knew him.

He wondered what she would have made of the man he'd been this week. Stepping out as the public face of his company, he'd felt more like himself than he could have once believed possible. He'd owned his achievements and his challenges—and the world kept spinning on its axis.

But his axis, that had already changed, on a moonlit night in the Outback, wrapped in her arms.

CHAPTER 12

*A*urora hung up her mother's old landline phone. Davey sounded brighter. He'd earned his phone privileges after a month at the rehabilitation center and wanted to check in on how the festival had gone. She'd been happy to report on that but fobbed off his query about Ryan with "it's complicated". Expecting some push back, she'd been surprised at his "you'll work it out, sis. I'm through underestimating you". It warmed a little of the chill inside.

The end of the festival had left her struggling with new realities. Life had changed and so had she. Ryan wasn't coming back. Nor was Davey.

Even her mum had conceded on the phone that her cruise trip had opened her eyes to making adjustments, as Aurora had hoped, including moving to a milder climate for her health, perhaps on the coast or nearer to her sister in Sydney. She was due home tomorrow, so Aurora was freshening up the house for her.

She hadn't heard from Ryan, but once she'd seen her mum, she planned a road trip. She'd had new tires fitted to the Mazda and the tank was full. Face to face, she would put herself on the line. She wasn't the same person she was before he came to town. She didn't underestimate her ability to do whatever she needed to do to make sure he knew she loved him.

He could still reject her, but that was outside her control, like so much of what happens in life. She wasn't about to let ten years pass this time before she had her answer.

A distant rumble had her searching the clear sky for thunderclouds, until it dawned on her the sound was man-made and growing louder. Her heart began to race, and she walked to the open front door.

A black motorbike swung around the corner, cruised down the street, and rolled to a stop in the driveway.

Her heart felt like it was pounding loud enough to be heard in the ensuing silence.

Ryan tilted his visor up. "Hey, Red. Got a minute?" His ice-blue eyes were guarded.

She wanted to throw herself into his arms, but she wasn't about to make it that easy.

"We've been over this. It's Aurora. If you can't get that right, I've got nothing to say to you, Ryan Harrington."

He huffed out a laugh. "You'll always be Red to me, Red." And he smiled a slow sexy smile that sent a familiar buzz lower in her belly. "But I'll call you whatever you want if you come for a ride with me."

"Just like that?"

"Yeah, just like that. Please?"

Emotions fizzed in her veins and something else entirely began to thrum in her limbs. She pulled the door closed behind her and walked down the steps. Ryan handed her a helmet and she pulled it on. He eased forward and she slid onto the bike wondering if she was crazy but deciding not to think too hard for now.

Besides, hot man, throbbing machine, it made her feel like

a rebel and a bad girl. She liked it. She was now the kind of woman who jumped at the chance to make bad decisions and ride dangerous motorcycles with hot men. Well, one hot man. She wrapped her arms around his waist, and he held them tightly in place for a moment before turning the bike and gunning the engine.

The curtains in the house across the road twitched as they peeled off down the drive.

He'd grown up with that, Aurora realized. No wonder he'd avoided attention since.

At the end of the street, Ryan turned, and she leaned with him.

They rode a short distance to the top of a hill, the quietest part of a quiet town. She hadn't visited the cemetery in a while, though her Mum did, maintaining her husband's grave.

Ryan rode the motorbike up under a shady gum tree and turned off the engine. They dismounted and shed their helmets, putting them on the bike. The calming familiar scent of the bush soothed Aurora as she took in the setting. Ryan held out a hand to her.

"I've never been here. I didn't think I'd ever visit. I'm ready now."

They walked along the rows of gravestones, eventually finding one that was newly erected. The inscription was simple, his father's name, dates of birth and death. And another line: *Survived by a son, Ryan Harrington.*

They stood, hands clasped, for what seemed like a long time. The day was hot, and a gust of wind stirred the leaves of the gum trees on the cemetery's perimeter. A single mournful crow cawed.

Ryan let out a sigh. When he spoke, his voice was grim.

"My dad was a shit dad. I couldn't wait to get out of this place, and I swore I wouldn't come back. After I left, I phoned, but dad was an abusive drunk. It never ended well."

She squeezed his hand, hoping that it would provide some small measure of comfort.

"He died a bitter old man. He never got over my mum leaving. He never stopped blaming me for it. I was a five-year-old kid when she left, I barely remember her. Any feelings I have about her are all crowded out by the feelings I had for him.

"He was my world. He tried his best at first, but by the time I was ten he was just mean and drunk, or hungover and mean, or occasionally sober for a bit, but I could never trust it to last ... You get the picture."

Aurora's heart ached. For that little boy and for the man blinking fast to stem the moisture pooling in his eyes.

"I'm so sorry, Ryan. Did anyone know?"

He shook his head. "I got pretty good at covering for him."

He cleared his throat and paused a moment before he could continue.

"He'd send me into the grocery store with ten bucks. I ate a lot of cereal and baked beans. People tried to help, but he ran them off, didn't like being judged. 'Bloody do-gooders' he called them.

"Your mum guessed a fair bit more than I let on. One of the reasons I ate so many meals at your place. But she never made a fuss about it, which I appreciated. He had me convinced that child services would send me to juvenile detention for a long time if they ever came to see how we lived."

"That's terrible."

Ryan lifted a shoulder and dropped it. "Sometimes I wondered if it might have been better. But then I'd think of your family and my other friends, the footy team, and I'd keep out of his way, camp up on the hill 'til things improved. Besides, he needed me."

Her heart clenched at the sadness in his voice. No child should have to experience that kind of heartbreak.

Ryan let go of her hand and crouched down, running his fingers over the lettering on the headstone.

"Sometimes I can't believe he's gone. I have a bad day and I think about him. What a waste of a life, you know?" He looked at her, pain etched on his face.

She knew this story was his real secret, not his out-of-the-limelight career. No one carried around this kind of burden without it affecting them every day. Whatever happened between them, she was glad he was telling her and that she could be there for him.

He picked up a fallen twig and twirled it, the brown gum leaves rustling, and stood looking down the hill toward the town. He'd been keeping this inside for too long. And there was nowhere she'd rather be than here, her presence helping him process the past.

When he spoke again, his voice was rough with emotion, and she pressed her fingernails into her palm to keep herself from breaking down. This wasn't about her.

"I never thought I'd regret not coming home when he died, but I do. He had enough pension money left to cover the cost of the burial. I thought there was nothing to come back for. There was no funeral."

He turned to look at her, regret shadowing his eyes.

"I should have come back, to see your mum, say goodbye, forgive him so I could move on. At the time, I was still too angry with him."

"You did what you thought was best," she ventured.

"Yeah. But I realized lately that I owe him. He showed me what I don't want. I don't want to be like him. Hating him pushed me to succeed at first, and then I just kept at it …

working, building the businesses, keeping people at a distance. I stopped hating him a long time ago, but I didn't make room for love." He tossed the twig to the barren ground.

"He knew you loved him."

"Maybe." He shrugged. "I didn't think I was capable of it. How could I have something I couldn't trust? But lately I've realized I was wrong about that, very wrong. I've been blessed to have some incredible people in my life, who support me and believe in me and want the best for me. I've had family all along, just never my own. I never believed I could have that."

"Oh, Ryan."

He wiped his hands against his eyes and swallowed, the muscles on his throat working. When he looked at her again, his face was resolved, and she held her breath, braced for what he would say next, nerves as taut as wire.

"When I came back and found you, I started feeling things for you that scared the hell out of me. I did a lot of things wrong, and I'm sorry for all the mistakes I made not being straight with you from the start. Aurora, I regret a lot of things. I don't want losing you to be one of them. I love you."

I love you. I love you. His words echoed in her head. He loved her? Ryan Harrington loved her!

Unaware of the turmoil his words had caused, he forged on.

"I'm new to love, probably going to make lots of mistakes. But I need to know. Is there a chance for us?"

He was looking at her with such seriousness, tension radiating off him in waves, as he held himself in check waiting for her answer. Whatever she said, she knew he'd respect her wishes. She was so glad for him that after everything he'd dealt with, he'd accepted his past enough to be willing to risk being vulnerable. Lucky for him, he'd chosen the woman who'd been in love with him as long as she could remember. Her.

She smiled at him and reached her hands up around his neck. His face was so filled with naked yearning that if she weren't already so deeply in love with him, she would have fallen then, hard.

Happiness overwhelmed her, a feeling as vast as the Outback sky, or it's rivers in flood.

"Chance is not a factor, Ryan. I love you too. I thought I loved you a long time ago, but that was just a hint of what I feel now. You're my man—heart, body, and soul. So, kiss me like you mean it."

Ryan's eyes crinkled and his lips curved in a wide smile of pure joy and hope, focused on her. A shiver of delight ran through her as he pulled her to him.

He lowered his lips but paused first.

"Yes, boss."

They kissed then, a kiss that flared with heat she knew would always be there between them, ready to flame into passion. But as Ryan claimed her lips like he claimed her heart, there was no place she wanted to be but in his arms.

HE END.

THANKS FOR READING RYAN'S RETURN

I hope you enjoyed reading Ryan and Aurora's story as much as I loved writing it. I love connecting with readers. If you like to stay in touch, find me at www.sarahartland.com on facebook at Sara Hartland Author or Instagram @inthehartland. Sign up to my newsletter to learn about my next book and to get a free short story. *His New Year's Wish* is a second chance rural romance about a sexy cattleman reconnecting with a woman from his past. Can one magic night change everything? Sign up and you'll find out.

ACKNOWLEDGMENTS

Thanks for cover design to Exposed Publishing, formatting to Ree Thornton, editing to Amanda Ashby, proofreading to Amy Hart Proofreading and mentorship to Rachel Bailey. All are extraordinary women dedicated to bringing out the best in others.

Heartfelt thanks to the most supportive writing group in the world, Writers Not Waiters (because if you're waiting for inspiration, you're a waiter not a writer) especially Josie Baker, Dana Mitchell, LJ Langdon, Elsa Holland, and Ree Thornton. With you, all things became possible.

Special thanks to Romance Writers of Australia Inc for supporting aspiring, emerging and established romance authors to be the best they can be. Congratulations on 30 years of service in 2021.

Romanceaustralia.com